the new *Lucinda*

By GRACE GELVIN KISINGER

Cover Design by Barbara Fox

SCHOLASTIC **SBS** BOOK SERVICES

Published by Scholastic Book Services, a division
of Scholastic Magazines, Inc., New York, N.Y.

Copyright © 1958 by Grace Gelvin Kisinger. This Scholastic
Book Services edition is published by arrangement with Thomas
Nelson & Sons.

1st printing . . . . . December 1963

Printed in the U.S.A.

TO MY SISTER
Peggy
WITH LOVE

C H A P T E R

1

CINDY TAYLOR WAS BORED. She was tired of the weather—of the drab sameness of the cold, dark January days; she was tired of school, with its unvarying routine of classes and homework; most of all, she was tired of herself and the dull, dateless, unexciting life she led.

"Cheer up, it's always this way in January," she told herself, as she laid fresh napkins beside the three place settings on the dining-room table. But she knew that there was more to her depression than the usual postholiday letdown. Even before Christmas, she had been restless and unhappy.

She straightened the centerpiece, frowned at it absently, and returned to the kitchen. "The table's set," she told her mother. "Anything else?"

"No, that's all for now." Mrs. Taylor looked up from

1

the bowl of cream she was whipping. "Your father called to say that he'd been detained by an important conference, so dinner will be late this evening. Don't you have any homework?"

"Only a little." Cindy's tone was listless. "And I don't feel like starting it now. I'll do it after dinner. I don't have anything else to do tonight."

She wandered into the living room and sank into one of the fireside chairs. "And that's the trouble," she thought dispiritedly. "I don't have anything else to do—tonight or tomorrow night or any other night. I'm sixteen years old but, for all that ever happens to me, I might as well be sixty!"

She leaned forward, cupping her chin in her hands and staring moodily into the fire. She was a tall girl, very slender, and she wore her blond hair long, pulled back in a ponytail. Wide-set blue eyes and a delicately modeled nose and chin gave her face a fragile look which would have been appealing were it not for the frown which creased her forehead and the downward droop of her lips.

"What's wrong with me?" she asked herself disconsolately. "I've spent all of my life right here in Exeter and I should have dozens of friends, but I haven't. None of the boys ever looks at me twice, and even the girls forget about me most of the time. When it comes down to it, the only real friend I have is Sally Baird. Sally says that I'm too shy and reserved, but how can I be anything else, looking the way I do?

Lucinda 'Beanpole' Taylor—the girl who didn't know when to stop growing—that's me!"

Sighing, Cindy looked away from the fire. Her glance fell on a magazine on the table beside her chair, and she saw that it was the latest issue of a smart periodical which her mother had received as a Christmas gift. Bold letters on the cover announced the lead article:

A NEW YEAR AND A NEW YOU!
MAKE YOURSELF INTO THE PERSON YOU WOULD LIKE TO BE

"The person I would like to be," Cindy thought wistfully. "Well, let's see . . . in the first place I'd lop off about four inches and be a nice, average five feet four. And then I'd change my coloring; instead of being a pale, washed-out blonde, I'd be a striking brunette or redhead. And of course I'd change my personality. I'd stop being self-conscious and uncertain; I'd be witty and clever and poised, and I'd always know exactly the right thing to say and do."

Thinking about her shortcomings, Cindy idly picked up the magazine, turned to the opening page, and was confronted by color photographs of two beautiful girls. Her glance went to the caption under the first picture. "Would you guess that this girl was forty pounds overweight two months ago?" it read. Disappointed, she slumped in her chair. She had been hoping for something different but it was the old familiar lose-weight Cinderella story. Streamline your figure and have the

3

world at your feet! Count your calories and you'll soon be counting compliments! She had read and heard it all, a thousand times before.

But then her eyes wandered to the other photograph and suddenly she caught her breath. "Margaret was drab in appearance, uninteresting even to herself, before she resolved to make herself into a fascinating person" read the legend. And the girl in the photograph *was* fascinating. Softly waved, gold-brown hair framed a lovely, serene face, with regular, delicate features and wide violet-blue eyes.

"Why, she looks a little like me," Cindy thought, startled. "Or what I'd like to look like." Straightening in her chair, she turned eagerly to the story. Margaret, it seemed, was far more of a problem to the author, who conducted a well-known school for models, than was Helen, the fat girl. For Helen was jolly and so large that no one could overlook her. But Margaret was shy and retiring. She had all of the necessary ingredients of a beauty but they were subdued. She was taught to "stand tall," to do her hair in a deceptively simple way that drew attention to her regular profile, to widen her mouth with lipstick, and to wear colors that brought out the color of her eyes—blues, violets, blacks, and grays, instead of the drab browns, beiges, and tans she had been wearing.

But the change in Margaret did not end with the improvement in her appearance. She was taught to speak slowly and distinctly in a relaxed voice rather

4

than in her usual nervous, high-pitched tones which betrayed inner anxiety. And she was taught to hide her nervousness behind a façade of serenity. By assuming an air of sophistication, beauty, and self-confidence, Margaret had put her new personality across within two months.

Cindy reread the last paragraph and slowly lowered the magazine to her lap. How wonderful to be made over into an entirely new and different person like that! She looked down at her taupe skirt and beige sweater, then rose and peered at herself in the mirror over the mantel. True, these shades of brown did nothing for anyone with blue eyes, but the colors had been popular last fall.

"I shouldn't have bought them for that reason," she thought. "The article's right—I ought to stick to colors that are becoming to me, regardless of what the other kids are wearing. And I shouldn't wear my hair in a ponytail, just because so many other girls do. It doesn't suit me because I'm so tall. It hasn't done me any good to try to conform, anyway. If only—"

But that was ridiculous. Everyone in Exeter would howl if Lucinda Taylor tried to make herself over. She had been born here and every grownup in town remembered the delicate baby, the timid little girl whose stage fright at a Sunday-school Christmas program almost ruined the show. Everyone in the junior and senior class—yes, and in the sophomore class, too— probably remembered Jimmy Albright's protest to Miss

Regina Smith at the Friday afternoon children's dancing class, six years ago: "No, I won't dance with that old beanpole, Cindy Taylor, and neither will any of the other guys; she walks all over our feet."

"Beanpole" Taylor. The nickname had clung. And how could a girl known as "Beanpole" even *hope* to change her personality without becoming the laughingstock of the town?

Sighing, Cindy placed the magazine on the table as she heard the family car turn into the drive.

She knew as soon as her father came into the house that something out-of-the-ordinary had happened. Henry Taylor was a tall and rather heavy-set man whose dark hair held only a sprinkling of gray and whose manner was normally calm and easygoing. But tonight he had an air of suppressed excitement. It was evident in the way he walked, in the extra sparkle in his eyes, even in the way he tweaked Cindy's ponytail as he greeted her. He went into the kitchen and closed the door and, for the next several minutes, she could hear him and her mother talking in low, excited-sounding voices. But she couldn't hear what they were saying.

They kept her in suspense until dinner was almost over. Then, when dessert was on the table, her father suddenly turned to his wife and said, "Shall we tell Cindy?"

"Tell me what?" Cindy wanted to know.

6

"Your father has news for you, Lucinda," her mother replied. "I think he'd like to tell you himself."

He nodded, smiling. "To make a long story short, Cindy, you are now looking at the glass company's new sales manager. Word of the promotion just came through today—that's what the conference was about."

"You mean you're the new *national* sales manager?" Cindy squeaked.

"Right." Her father's smile broadened. "You understand, of course, that it means leaving Exeter and moving to Woodmont where the company has its main offices. They want me there as soon as possible, so we'll have to put the house up for sale immediately."

"It shouldn't be too hard to find a buyer," Mrs. Taylor said thoughtfully. "The problem will be to find a house in Woodmont that we like as well. But we may be lucky. I hope so. I'd like to be moved and settled before the end of the month."

Dismayed, Cindy stared at her mother and then at her father. How could they talk so calmly about leaving Exeter? Didn't they realize what it would mean to her? True, she wasn't popular here, but at least she knew everyone and everyone knew her. "And I do like my courses in school," she thought. "And there's Sally. What will I ever do without her? I'll be lost in a strange town!"

Her parents were still talking about the impending move. Suddenly Mrs. Taylor interrupted herself and turned again to Cindy. "Don't forget to ask for a

7

transcript of your grades, Lucinda. Perhaps you'd better speak to your teachers about it tomorrow, so that it will be ready by the time we leave. And I do hope you will enjoy living in Woodmont."

"But I don't know anyone there!" Cindy protested weakly.

"You will," her father assured her. "Unless I miss my guess, you'll feel right at home there within a few months."

"I hope so," Cindy murmured. Privately, however, she didn't share her father's optimism. Other girls could do it. Other girls could move to a strange town and know everyone in the place within a matter of weeks. But not "Beanpole" Taylor. It would probably take her forever to make even one friend.

When the dinner dishes were done, Cindy went up to her room to study. She paused on the way, however, to pick up the magazine she had been reading before dinner and, once in her room, she stretched across her bed and turned again to the picture of Margaret. She stared at the lovely, serene face, the softly waved hair, the violet-blue eyes. It was hard to believe that this girl had ever been dull or plain or uninteresting. But she had been. According to the article, she had once been almost as dull and plain and uninteresting as Cindy Taylor.

Suddenly Cindy's eyes widened. Maybe, after all, there was a silver lining to this move to a strange town!

She sat up and swung her feet over the edge of the bed. Why not? She couldn't make herself over in Exeter, but in Woodmont, where nobody would know her or know what she'd been like before, why couldn't she do what Margaret had done? Why couldn't she change her appearance and personality and be what she wanted to be?

She stood up, went to her mirror, and looked grimly at her reflection. Slumped shoulders, a habit she had acquired in an effort to make herself look shorter; hair pulled back in that absurd and unbecoming ponytail; plain beige sweater, which did absolutely nothing for her coloring—

"You look like an overgrown twelve-year-old!" she told herself accusingly.

But she didn't have to look that way, did she? What if she, like Margaret, were to stand straight and tall? What if she changed her hair style and make-up and switched to more becoming colors in her clothes?

It shouldn't really be too difficult to change her appearance. But what about her personality? If everything went according to plan, they would be moving to Woodmont by the end of the month—perhaps before then. No one could change her personality in that short a time, could she?

Frowning at her mirrored reflection, Cindy thought of the conclusion of the magazine story. By assuming an air of sophistication, beauty, and self-confidence,

Margaret had put her new personality across within two months.

By *assuming* an air of sophistication, Cindy repeated uncertainly to herself. "I wonder if I could do it? I wonder if I could pretend to be poised and sophisticated and do it convincingly enough to make everyone in Woodmont believe that's what I really am?"

Half an hour later, when her mother came to the door of her bedroom, Cindy was still standing before the mirror. She had untied the ponytail and parted her hair, and was holding it back from her face. Her eyes were half closed and her head was tilted backward.

"You've been so quiet that I came up to see if anything is wrong," Mrs. Taylor said anxiously. "I hope you're not upset about leaving Exeter, Lucinda. Your father and I would both be worried if we thought you minded very much."

Cindy turned dreamily toward her mother. "Mind?" she said in a low, musical voice. "No, I don't mind. Why should I? Before we go, though, I think I'll have my hair cut."

C H A P T E R

2

THREE WEEKS LATER, Cindy sat in the study hall in Room 304 of the Woodmont High School. A physics textbook lay open on the desk before her, but Cindy's mind was far from the world of molecules and atoms and textbook problems. It was on a much more immediate problem of her own: Would she be able to put it over? Would she be able to convince her new schoolmates here in Woodmont that she was poised, self-confident, and sophisticated when, in reality, she wasn't anything of the kind?

"May I borrow your eraser for a minute, please?" The soft whisper from across the aisle interrupted Cindy's thoughts. Turning, she saw Rose Walsh looking directly at her.

Cindy picked up her eraser and handed it across the aisle, doing her best to appear casual, but she was conscious of a sudden tremor of excitement. Although this was her first day in Woodmont High, she had already noticed that the attractive, dark-haired Rose seemed to be very popular with the boys.

"I'll bet she's always been popular," Cindy thought, watching Rose as she erased something from her tablet. "She looks like the sort of girl who's always had lots of attention."

"Thanks a million." Rose returned the eraser with a careless smile and Cindy tried hard to make her answering smile equally noncommittal. If she hoped to create the right sort of impression here, she mustn't seem too eager.

Someone at the back of the study hall rose and walked down the aisle past her desk. She glanced up and then looked swiftly down at her book again. It was Malcolm Gordon, son of the vice-president of the company which had transferred her father to Woodmont. Cindy had not yet met Malcolm—or Mack, as everyone called him—but in one day she had secretly decided that he was the most handsome boy in Woodmont High.

She kept her eyes fastened on her book until he was well past her desk but presently, hearing the hum of the pencil sharpener, she risked another upward glance.

Because he was so tall, Mack had to bend slightly to use the sharpener. Most people would have looked awkward in such a position, but not Mack. Gazing through the window at the gray January sky, with a faraway look in his eyes, he seemed completely unself-conscious.

But Cindy was sure that most of the girls were watching him. Who could help watching Mack? Who could help noticing how beautifully the impeccably tailored sports jacket fitted his broad shoulders, or the way his blond hair shone under the fluorescent ceiling lights?

The sound of the sharpener ceased, and Cindy's eyes returned hurriedly to her book again. If Mack happened to glance her way, she wouldn't want him to catch her staring at him. Poised, sophisticated girls didn't stare at boys. They let boys stare at them instead.

She couldn't help wondering, as Mack again passed her desk, if he had noticed her. It wasn't entirely impossible, was it, especially since she was wearing her best sweater and her new gray skirt? It would have been better, of course, if her mother had let her wear the gold clip earrings—the ones Sally had given her for Christmas.

But Mrs. Taylor had been adamant about the earrings. "Not for school, Lucinda. They're inappropriate."

Inappropriate? Well, Rose Walse was wearing earrings and they didn't seem to be detracting from *her* appearance.

"But if I can't, I can't," Cindy thought, absently brushing a fleck of chalk dust from her skirt. "At least, thank goodness, I'm allowed to wear lipstick. If the

13

subject of earrings ever comes up, I'll just have to pretend I don't care for them."

The warning buzzer sounded which meant that only three minutes remained before the end of the final period, and Cindy closed her physics book and smoothed her short hair. So far she had been too busy enrolling in her various classes to have an opportunity to try out her new personality but now, at the end of the school day, it was time to begin. As soon as the final bell rang, she would return to her home room and deliberately linger at her desk, pretending to be sorting books. Surely, if she did, some of her new classmates would approach her. And then she would have a chance to make some of the remarks she had rehearsed so painstakingly last night at home. Casual, sophisticated-sounding remarks which, if she remembered to say them in exactly the right tone of voice, would be bound to make an impression.

The bell rang, marking the end of the period, and Cindy gathered up her books and went quickly down the aisle. At the door, she paused and glanced back in time to see that Rose Walsh had been joined by Mack Gordon; then, turning, she hurried along the corridor toward her home room.

Head down, her mind intent on her plan, she didn't see the slender, dark-haired boy who was striding toward her from the opposite direction, calling something over his shoulder. Nor, apparently, did he see her.

They collided in the middle of the corridor and the force of the collision sent Cindy's books sailing to the floor.

"Oh say, I'm sorry!" With an apologetic smile, the boy knelt to pick up her books. "Wasn't watching where I was going. I hope you're not hurt."

"Not at all." Just in time, Cindy remembered to make her voice indifferent. "It's really my fault as much as yours. I wasn't watching where I was going, either."

The boy stood up and she saw that he was an inch or two taller than she—about five feet nine or ten, she guessed. He handed her the books.

"Say," he said slowly, "you're new around here, aren't you?"

Cindy carefully replaced her books under her arm. Take it easy, she warned herself. "Yes," she replied in her new low voice. "This is my first day. My family and I moved here last Saturday. I'm a junior and my name's Cindy Taylor."

"And I'm Peter Holmes, a senior." He regarded her quizzically through his shell-rimmed glasses. "Cindy, h'm? Let's see—blue eyes, blond hair, a nice straight nose, and two, no three, freckles—yes, I agree. You do look like Cinderella."

"It isn't Cindy-short-for-Cinderella. It's Cindy-short-for-Lucinda." In spite of her determination not to blush, Cindy could feel her cheeks turning warm. "I was named for my paternal grandmother." Now why had she thought it necessary to tell him that?

"I see." Peter's smile widened. "How do you like it here, Cindy-short-for-Lucinda? Having any trouble finding your way around?"

"No." Cindy hesitated and had a sudden inspiration. "After all, it's not a large school." Actually, of course, Woodmont High was almost twice as large as Exeter High, but there was no need to tell Peter Holmes so, was there?

Behind his glasses, Peter's brown eyes had taken on a somewhat crestfallen look. "Well," he said awkwardly, "let me know if there's anything I can do to help."

"I will." Cindy hurried on, a little embarrassed by the encounter but encouraged, too. Peter Holmes seemed like a friendly sort of boy. Too bad he wasn't better-looking. Of course it would have been much more exciting if it had been Mack Gordon she'd run into. But at least, judging from his manner, she had managed to make an impression on Peter. Now if she could only make the same kind of an impression on some of the others—

But when she arrived at her home room, she found it deserted except for Miss Ferguson, the English teacher, who was sitting at her desk looking over some papers. Apparently the encounter with Peter Holmes had delayed Cindy a few minutes too long.

Swallowing her disappointment, she went to her desk to put away her books, except the two she wanted to take home. She was starting for the locker room when Miss Ferguson suddenly looked up.

16

"You're a little late, aren't you, Lucinda?"

"Yes." Cindy paused beside the teacher's desk. "I ran into somebody in the hall and we stopped to talk."

"Oh." Miss Ferguson smiled. "I was looking over the transcript of your Exeter credits a while ago, and I notice that you've made consistently high grades in English. Do you like the subject?"

"Yes, I do." Forgetting her pose, Cindy spoke sincerely. "Especially English composition. I've always liked to write."

"And do you like to read, too?"

"Very much."

The teacher nodded. "I thought so." She was silent for a moment. "Well, Lucinda, I'm looking forward to having you in English III. It's always rewarding to come across an interested student. So keep up the good work, won't you?"

"I will." Cindy smiled at Miss Ferguson and went on her way, thinking to herself that it would be impossible for her *not* to work hard in English when she liked it so well. However, she would have to be careful about showing too much enthusiasm for schoolwork when she was around her contemporaries. It wouldn't do to let them know that she was actually a diligent and conscientious student.

Outdoors, although the weather was warmer than it had been at noon, everything was tinged with the somber gray of late January. Giant clouds of dirty

17

gray hung like heavy blankets in the sky, obscuring the pale winter sunlight. Patches of gunmetal-colored ice, all that remained of this morning's snow, lay in scattered heaps on the gray-brown earth. Even the limbs of the trees had a grayish look, like the spikes of an ancient iron fence.

Three girls were standing at the foot of the broad shallow steps which led to the high school building. As Cindy paused to button her coat, she recognized them and immediately began to breathe a little faster. All three were juniors and she had already observed that they seemed to be among the most popular girls in the class. Exactly the sort with whom Cindy most wanted to associate!

Hoping against hope that they would notice her, she fixed a remote expression on her face and sauntered down the steps, doing her best to imitate the nonchalant, unconcerned walk of a model.

The tallest of the three girls turned and smiled. "Oh, hello there! I was hoping we'd run into you and have a chance to get acquainted. I'm Martha Alexander."

"I'm Cindy Taylor." Returning the smile, Cindy strolled over to the group.

"Yes, I know." Martha's round face broke into a friendly grin. "We all know who you are, since you're new here and there's only one of you. But there are so many of us, I think we ought to give you a fighting chance to remember our names. This is Susan Greer," motioning to the red-haired, freckled-faced girl at her

18

side. "And this is Jan Harris." She indicated the slender brunette who was the third member of the trio.

Susan and Jan both nodded. "Hi," they said simultaneously.

"Hi." Cindy managed to speak calmly but it was harder than she'd thought it would be to hide her instinctive friendliness.

All three girls were eying her with unabashed curiosity. "How do you feel after your first day in Woodmont High?" asked Susan. "Think you're going to like it here?"

"I think so," Cindy replied. "It seems very nice. I mean," she went on hastily, "for a small school."

"Oh," said Susan.

There was a short pause.

"Where did you live before you moved here?" Jan wanted to know.

"Exeter. That's in the northern part of the state." It suddenly occurred to Cindy that Exeter wasn't so far away but that some Woodmont High students might have visited there, so she added quickly, "It's a small town and a small school, but I've traveled a good bit with my parents." Well, she had taken a Great Lakes cruise with them two years ago, hadn't she, when her father's district had won first place in the sales contest? And there had been a motor trip to Canada four years ago, when she was twelve.

This time it was Jan who said, "Oh."

There was another short silence. "We were thinking

of going down to Weyman's Drugstore for a Coke," Martha said hesitantly. "You wouldn't by any chance care to join us, would you?"

"I'd love to!" Cindy exclaimed impulsively. A second later she could have kicked herself. She'd sounded too eager. If she hoped to make an impression on them, she mustn't let them see that she was *anxious* to make friends.

Fortunately, the other three didn't seem to notice her enthusiasm. Linking her arm through Cindy's, Martha said, "Let's go, then. We can talk in the drugstore."

Weyman's Drugstore looked very much like Sloane's, back in Exeter. There were the same long rows of neatly labeled jars and bottles, the same glass-topped counters piled high with cleansing tissues, tooth pastes, and mouthwashes, and, over it all, the same faintly perfumed, faintly medicinal smell. The only difference was that the booths in the Exeter drugstore had been old-fashioned high-backed ones, while here they were low and made of plastic and chrome.

When the four girls were seated in one of the booths, Susan changed her mind about ordering a Coke and decided to have a chocolate sundae instead.

"She always does," Martha said, laughing. "You might as well get used to it, Cindy. Sue has an appetite like a horse—although I swear I don't know where she puts everything."

Cindy grinned in spite of herself. Small, red-haired Susan did look as though she existed on a diet of lettuce

20

leaves and not much else. Martha, on the other hand, looked quite capable of holding her own at any dinner table. Not that she was fat, or even plump, but she had the kind of tall, well-rounded figure and pink, glowing cheeks that made you think instinctively of the phrase, "picture of health." Dark-haired, quiet-voiced Jan Harris was the in-between one—a girl of average height and weight.

"They're nice," Cindy thought, studying her companions covertly while she pretended to pore over the menu. "And pretty, too. It's easy to see why they're popular. But they're probably particular about the people they run around with. I'll have to careful of what I say and do if I hope to make an impression on them."

A waitress came to take their orders and went away again, and Jan leaned forward, smiling. "That's a darling sweater, Cindy. Did you buy it in Exeter?"

Pleased, Cindy darted a quick glance at her sweater. It had been a Christmas present from one of her aunts, and this was the second time she had worn it. "No, it came from New York," she replied with simulated indifference.

Jan blinked. "How wonderful to be able to shop in New York!"

Cindy pretended to stifle a yawn. Well, the sweater *had* come from New York; her aunt had ordered it from a department-store holiday catalogue.

Beside Cindy in the booth, Martha stirred suddenly.

"Tell us something about Exeter, why don't you, Cindy?"

Cindy turned to her. "What would you like to know?"

"For instance, what did you do for fun there?"

Cindy hesitated. Careful, she warned herself. This is important. Better not go into too much detail or they might ask questions you'd have trouble answering. She made her voice elaborately casual. "Oh, the usual things. Dances, parties, dates, football games. *You* know."

The other three girls looked at each other.

"What are the boys in Exeter like?" asked Susan.

"Oh, about average, I'd say." Cindy did her best to sound worldly-wise and experienced. "Bob Evans, last year's senior class president, was quite good-looking, though. And a terrific dancer." It was true. Bob Evans *was* good-looking and, according to all reports, a terrific dancer. Of course he'd scarcely been aware of a sophomore named "Beanpole" Taylor, but there was no need to say so, was there?

Martha, Jan, and Susan looked impressed. "The senior class president?" Jan repeated slowly.

"Yes." Cindy managed to achieve exactly the right offhand tone. Afraid that she might be pressed for details of her non-existent dates with Bob Evans, she hurried on. "And some of the boys in the mixed chorus were all right. We used to have quite a lot of fun at rehearsals." This much, at least, was strictly the truth. Cindy loved to sing and she had always enjoyed the chorus rehearsals. Some of the boys had been good-looking, although none of them had ever paid much attention to Cindy or her friend, Sally Baird.

"What about the girls?" Martha wanted to know. "There must be some cute girls there, aren't there?"

"Some," Cindy drawled. "Of course, those of us who were dating didn't bother much with those who didn't. You know how it is."

"Yes, I know." Martha's tone was odd and so was the glance she exchanged with Jan and Susan.

There was a silence. Then Jan said quietly, "I'm glad you sing. We don't have a mixed chorus here, but we do have a girls' Glee Club. Martha and Susan and I belong and we enjoy it, although I can't honestly say it's particularly exciting. However, if you think you'd like to join, we'd be glad to give your name to Miss Clarke, the director."

"I wouldn't mind." Elated, Cindy pressed her hands together under the table to keep their sudden trembling from showing. It was working! She'd impressed Martha and Jan and Susan so much that they were already trying to think of ways to include her in their activities. "When do you meet?" she asked.

"On Wednesdays at four," answered Martha. "So the next rehearsal will be the day after tomorrow. If you want me to, I'll speak to Miss Clarke and see if she can arrange an audition for you before then."

"Fine," said Cindy happily.

A blast of cold air from the door made all the girls

turn their heads, and Cindy caught her breath. Rose Walsh was walking into the store with Mack Gordon and another boy. Rose was talking as they came in, swinging her shoulder-length hair from side to side as she looked up at first one and then the other of the two boys. Both Mack and the other boy were looking down at her with obvious admiration.

"And you certainly can't blame them," Cindy thought wistfully. "In that white leather jacket and red skirt, she looks like a girl on a magazine cover. You can see that she knows how to treat boys, too. Even if I were lucky enough to be in her place, I probably wouldn't be able to think of a word to say to them."

The other boy, Cindy noticed, was a little taller than Mack—about six feet two to Mack's six feet—but Mack was the more handsome of the two. In his beautifully tailored sports jacket and slacks, with a tweed topcoat slung carelessly over his shoulders, he was, Cindy decided, the best-looking boy she had ever seen in her life. He walked with the easy, self-assured stride of an athlete.

By the sudden silence in the booth, Cindy knew that Martha and Jan and Susan had also noticed the new arrivals. Were they expecting Rose and the two boys to join them? They were heading their way. Obviously they were going to have to sit *somewhere*.

CHAPTER

3

Rose caught sight of Cindy and her companions and paused beside their booth, with the boys a couple of steps behind her. "What's this?" she laughed. "An extra class meeting?"

"No, nothing like that." Martha's pink cheeks had turned a deeper pink. "We're just getting acquainted with Cindy."

"Oh yes, our new classmate." Rose's black eyes swept over Cindy appraisingly. "How do you like Woodmont?"

Cindy felt suddenly and unaccountably awkward. "Quite well, thank you," she murmured.

Mack and the other boy moved closer to the booth and glanced at her curiously. "That's right, Bill," said Mack. "We almost forgot that there's a new girl in town. Cute, too!" He grinned lazily at Cindy and turned to Rose. "Better look to your laurels, Rose, or you'll be losing your beauty crown!"

"So I see." Rose laughed lightly but she didn't look particularly amused. She tugged Mack's arm. "Well, come on, you two. I haven't finished that story yet." With a casual nod, she moved on past the booth, taking the two boys with her.

Martha, Jan, and Susan all began to talk at once, but it was several minutes before Cindy heard anything they were saying. She was too conscious of the low-pitched murmur of voices which came from the end booth where Rose and the two boys had seated themselves.

Suddenly she realized that Martha had asked her a question. "I'm sorry, Martha," she apologized. "What did you say?"

"I asked if you have any brothers or sisters."

"No, I'm an only child." Cindy hesitated for a second and then went on impulsively, "Rose Walsh is certainly attractive, isn't she?"

"Yes." Susan's tone was curt. Martha and Jan merely nodded. But the expression on their faces was so odd that for a moment, Ciny wondered whether she should drop the subject. Obviously they didn't want to talk about Rose. But why not? Surely they weren't jealous of her, were they? They couldn't be—not when they were so pretty and popular themselves. Besides, there were certain things Cindy was dying to know, and how could she find out if she didn't ask?

She cleared her throat. "Rose seems to be popular with the boys, too," she ventured. "Does she go steady with Mack?"

"Not with Mack," Jan said. "But she does date Bill Norberry, the other boy, quite often. And Bill and Mack are close pals."

"Oh? Then who is Mack's steady date?" Cindy held her breath, waiting for the answer.

"Mack?" Susan giggled and wrinkled her freckled nose. "Nobody in particular and everybody in general. To use Mack's own words, he likes to 'play the field.' End of quote."

It was the answer Cindy had been hoping to hear. Mentally hugging herself, she said, "I'm surprised somebody hasn't latched onto him. He's very good-looking, don't you think?"

"And very conceited," Susan returned dryly. "As for latching onto him, if you're getting any ideas of that, you'd better forget them. From all I hear, it would be like trying to latch onto greased lightning."

In her interest in Mack, Cindy had forgotten her pose, but Susan's words reminded her. "Oh goodness, I wouldn't dream of it," she said loftily. "I was just curious because Mack's father and mine happen to work for the same company."

"The glass company?" asked Martha. "Mack's father is the vice-president, isn't he?"

"Yes, and mine is the sales manager," Cindy said proudly. "I've heard him speak of the Gordons and that's why I asked about Mack." To change the subject, she went on, "By the way, I met one of the senior boys this afternoon. We accidentally ran into each other and almost knocked each other down. His name is Peter Holmes."

"Peter Holmes!" echoed Martha.

"Lucky you," Susan murmured.

"Why?" asked Cindy.

"Peter Holmes is one of the nicest boys in school," Jan stated emphatically. "I should warn you, though, that he doesn't bother much with girls."

"You mean he plays the field, like Mack?"

"No, he's definitely not like Mack," said Martha. "But he's the editor of the *Crimson Banner,* the school paper, which keeps him pretty busy. Anyway, he's never been the kind to run around much. More the serious type."

Cindy nodded. It was exactly the impression she'd formed of Peter. "He's certainly not very handsome."

"No," agreed Susan. "But don't let that mislead you. Most of the girls would be thrilled to have a date with Peter if he'd ask them."

The talk drifted to other things then. Much of the time, however, Cindy's mind remained on the three occupants of the end booth, and it was still on them when she and her companions finally got up to leave. She didn't turn around but she was careful to walk with her head high and her shoulders back in case Mack noticed her departure.

Before they separated at the corner, Martha and Jan

and Susan promised to arrange a glee club audition for Cindy before Wednesday, if possible. They were so gracious about it that Cindy had walked on for several blocks before she realized that they hadn't said anything to her about going to Weyman's with them again.

The Taylor's new house was in the Woodmont Park section of town, seven blocks beyond the business district. It wasn't literally a new house, for it was about ten years old, but Cindy thought that the ivy-covered brick and dignified colonial architecture were attractive. And, from her first glimpse, she'd been delighted by the proximity of the park's swimming pool and tennis courts. She had been a little disappointed to discover over the weekend that all of their immediate neighbors were either elderly people or young couples with small children. But she'd consoled herself with the thought that the lack of any teen-agers in the neighborhood wouldn't matter once she started to school.

Now, however, as she went inside and tossed her books on the vestibule table, Cindy again found herself wishing that some of her classmates lived nearby. How much easier everything would be if even one of them had happened to live next door for instance!

"But I'm going to have lots of friends," she reassured herself, determinedly shaking off her sudden pang of loneliness. "If I keep on making an impression, the way I did today, it probably won't be long until I'll be running around with Martha and Jan and Susan. And then I won't need to care about how far away they live."

She started to call out, announcing her arrival, then remembered that her mother had planned to go shopping this afternoon. A quick inspection of the downstairs rooms revealed that she had not yet returned. Cindy went to the bookcase, pulled out a book she had been reading before she left Exeter, and settled down with it in one of the living-room chairs. But, although she tried, she soon found that she couldn't keep her mind on the story. She kept thinking about Woodmont High School and the people she had met today. Peter Holmes, Rose Walsh, Miss Ferguson, Mack Gordon . . . Mack certainly seemed to be prominent in school. What had he been thinking in the drugstore, when he'd made that remark to Rose Walsh about losing her beauty crown? Had he really noticed Cindy and thought she was attractive, or had he just been teasing Rose?

And what about Rose? She was undeniably popular with the boys, but why didn't Martha and Jan and Susan like her?

"Or did I imagine it?" Cindy wondered. "I was tense and excited while we were in the drugstore. Maybe I simply imagined that they don't like her. Or maybe it's just a passing thing. Maybe they've had an argument of some kind with Rose and are temporarily giving her the cold shoulder."

After a while, Cindy closed her book and returned it to the bookcase. She wandered through the kitchen, helping herself to a pretzel on the way, and went downstairs to the basement recreation room.

The recreation room was another feature of the new house that had enchanted her on sight. It wasn't elaborate but it had an open fireplace and a battered but still usable Ping-pong table, left in the house by its former owner. Seeing the room for the first time, Cindy had begun to dream immediately of the parties she would give there. They would be gay, informal gatherings, presided over by a vivacious, confident hostess who would bear no resemblance whatever to the bashful, awkward "Beanpole" Taylor of old.

But could she put it over? It was true that she'd made a good start today and had apparently managed to convince Martha and Jan and Susan that she'd been the center of an admiring circle of friends in Exeter. But could she continue the pretense indefinitely?

"If only it didn't make me feel so peculiar," Cindy thought, frowning absently at some empty packing boxes in the corner. "There's no real reason for me to feel that way, is there, even if I did let Martha and the other girls assume some things that aren't true? After all, it isn't as though I'd told them an outright lie."

Nevertheless, she'd have to be careful about what she said to them from now on, or she would be forced into telling lies—to cover up. And that wouldn't do at all.

How had Margaret of the magazine article handled the problem? According to the author, Margaret had put her new personality across by *assuming* an air of sophistication, beauty, and self-confidence. But how far had she gone with the pretense? How had she known where to draw the line?

The Taylors' old porch glider had been placed in front of the fireplace. Cindy went over to it now and sat down, munching on her pretzel and debating the advisability of lighting a fire. She finally decided not to bother, reminding herself that by the time she had a fire going, her mother would probably be home and it would be time to start dinner preparations.

Thinking of her mother, Cindy sighed involuntarily, wondering why it was that she had inherited so many of her mother's physical characteristics without, apparently, any of her charm or poise. Mrs. Taylor was the sort of woman for whom butchers always saved their choicest cuts of meat and for whom delivery boys were always offering to run extra errands. It had been that way in Exeter and it would undoubtedly be that way in Woodmont, too. Of course she deserved peoples' admiration and affection for, in addition to being gay and pretty, she was innately warmhearted—the kind of woman who was always feeding stray dogs or going to the aid of a sick neighbor.

And Cindy's father was a genial man. For years he had been the glass company's leading salesman and, more recently, one of its most successful district managers. This latest promotion, Cindy knew, had been the logical next step up the ladder for him. And she was proud of him—of both of her parents. She wished that she were more like them.

"But I'm not like them," she thought, pulling absently at a loose button on one of the glider cushions. "They're always at ease with other people; neither one of them ever freezes up in a crowd the way I do. They never have the least bit of trouble making friends."

The front door slammed and, a moment later, the sound of light, quick footsteps overhead told Cindy that her mother was home. She waited for a few minutes, then went upstairs.

Mrs. Taylor was in the kitchen unpacking a bag of groceries. Cindy paused in the doorway, noticing how pretty her mother looked, even after what must have been a hard afternoon's shopping.

"Hi," she called. "Anything I can do to help?"

Mrs. Taylor jumped. "Oh, Cindy, you startled me! I didn't know you were home. But since you are, you might wash some of this lettuce for a salad."

"All right." Cindy unwrapped the lettuce and carried it to the sink. While she held it under the running water, she watched her mother, admiring the efficient way she went about her household tasks, admiring, too, her serene, unselfconscious beauty.

At thirty-nine, Anne Taylor had the slender figure and the clear, smooth skin of a girl in her twenties. Her hair, as fair as Cindy's, was untinged with gray and she wore it pinned in a neat chignon at the nape of her neck.

"Someday," Cindy thought, "I may let my hair grow long again and wear it that way. But will I ever have a personality like Mother's?"

Mrs. Taylor came over to the sink to draw water for the coffee. "How did everything go at school today?"

"Just fine," Cindy replied. She wished that she could ask her mother for advice about how to make friends, but she knew that she couldn't. She could ask her parents for advice about the little things, such as what to wear and which fork to use and the proper thing to say at a wedding reception. She could even ask them now and then about some specially bothersome problem in homework. But she couldn't, she simply *couldn't* ask them how to go about becoming popular.

She shook the last clinging drops of water from the lettuce and dried her hands on a paper towel. "By the way, I had a talk with Miss Ferguson, my new English teacher, today. She complimented me on my English grades in Exeter and said she hopes I'll keep on doing good work."

"That's wonderful, Lucinda. I hope you do, too." Her mother smiled. "How do you like your new classmates?"

"I like them very much. Three of the girls in my class —Martha Alexander and Jan Harris and Susan Greer— invited me to Weyman's Drugstore with them after school, and they were just as friendly as could be."

"I'm glad." Her mother measured coffee carefully into the percolator. "They must have taken an immediate liking to you, to invite you so soon. Sometimes people are a little slow about approaching strangers, you know."

"Yes, I know."

"Incidentally, Lucinda," Mrs. Taylor continued, "I was thinking earlier today that it would be nice to invite Sally down for a weekend soon. If you wanted to, you could have a party to introduce her to some of your new friends. Would you like that?"

"I'd love it!" Cindy replied spontaneously. Then, belatedly, she realized that, much as she was longing to see Sally, she couldn't carry out the suggestion if she hoped to continue in her new role. Sally wouldn't deliberately betray her; of course, she wouldn't call her "Beanpole," but what if she should accidentally let something slip to the Woodmont High crowd?

"It's too much of a risk to take," Cindy thought worriedly. "If they happened to mention Bob Evans, for instance, Sally might tell them that he never dated anyone but senior girls, and if that happened, I'd never be able to face these kids again."

Hoping to divert her mother's mind from the proposed visit, she said, "I met the Gordons' son today. His name's Malcolm, but everyone calls him Mack, and he's in my class. As a matter of fact, he and some other kids stopped to talk with us for a few minutes in the drugstore."

"Yes, I heard that their youngest son was still in high school," her mother remarked. "Oh, and that reminds me. We're invited there for dinner Wednesday night."

Cindy's mind was still on the drugstore scene. "Invited where?"

"To the Gordons'. Mrs. Gordon called me this morning."

"To the Gordons!"

"Yes. Don't let me forget to tell your father when he comes home, so that he won't make other plans for that evening."

"I'll remind you," said Cindy. She knew that there wasn't a chance that *she* would forget the invitation. The thought of being with Mack, of being his guest, was so exciting that it swept all her problems from her mind.

CHAPTER

4

MARTHA ALEXANDER TOLD Cindy the next day that the Glee Club audition had been arranged for Wednesday afternoon.

"You're to go directly to the auditorium at four," she said. "Miss Clarke said she'd be glad to audition you before the regular rehearsal."

"I'll be there," Cindy promised, doing her best to sound as though the thought of the audition didn't worry her in the least.

"Jan and Susan and I will try to get there early," Martha continued, "to introduce you to Miss Clarke and lend our moral support—if it's needed." Martha didn't, however, say anything to Cindy about getting together again after school, and neither did Jan or Susan.

And so, when Cindy's second day in Woodmont High

was over, she found herself walking home alone. She tried not to feel depressed, but she couldn't help wondering if she had unwittingly said or done something to detract from yesterday's auspicious beginning; try as she would, she couldn't think of a single thing. She had worn her gray skirt again today, but she'd exchanged yesterday's sweater for a fresh white blouse and she'd also worn her prettiest bracelet, so it was unlikely that anything had been wrong about her appearance. And she had been very careful, too, to maintain her pose of sophistication all day. Yet the fact remained that, except for her one brief talk with Martha, not one person had gone out of his or her way to say anything to Cindy today. Even Mack, contrary to her hopes and expectations, hadn't said a word to her about Wednesday night. In fact, he'd scarcely appeared to notice her today.

"But he may not know anything about the dinner," Cindy reassured herself, hurrying home through the cold winter afternoon. "It's quite possible that his mother forgot to mention it to him. He'll probably find out about it tonight and say something to me tomorrow."

Mack, however, continued to ignore Cindy when she saw him at school on Wednesday. Once again he appeared to be hardly aware of her presence in the class.

The Glee Club audition turned out to be far less of an ordeal than Cindy had feared. When she went to the auditorium after her last class, she found Martha and Jan and Susan waiting there for her. They introduced her to Miss Clarke, the young and pretty music supervisor, who made everything as easy as possible.

She took Cindy aside, out of the others' hearing, and asked her to sing some scales, and then she asked her to sight-read a few bars of music from several songs. By the time Cindy had finished the last one, the music teacher was smiling.

"That's fine, Lucinda," she said. "You don't have a strong voice but it's clear and true, and I'm ever so glad you're an alto." Then she assigned Cindy to the alto section and the audition was over. After the rehearsal, Martha and Jan and Susan again invited Cindy to Weyman's Drugstore with them.

"It proves that you shouldn't jump to conclusions," Cindy thought, accepting the invitation with an inner relief that was hard to conceal. "Here I was, afraid I'd done something wrong, and all the time I guess they were only busy with other things."

For a while, sitting in the drugstore, they talked about the rehearsal, and Cindy, who had enjoyed every minute of it, forgot her pose temporarily and joined eagerly and happily in the talk. And then, unexpectedly, the subject changed.

"I suppose it's too early to make definite plans," Susan Greer said, frowning thoughtfully, "but I've been asked to serve on the decorations committee for the junior prom in March, and I'd like to do something different this year." She turned to Cindy. "Since you

39

went to so many proms in Exeter, I was wondering if you might have some suggestions."

Cindy gulped. Racking her brain frantically for an idea, she thought of last year's senior prom which had been held in the Exeter High gym. She hadn't been invited to the dance, but she and Sally had purposely sneaked into the gym on the afternoon preceding the prom to peek at the decorations.

With an effort, she managed to sound offhand. "At last year's senior prom, they decorated the gym with balloons in purple and gold, the school colors. They were tied to the ceiling with purple and gold streamers and there was a girl's name in each balloon. Then, during one of the dances, they released the balloons and the boys had to catch and break them and dance the next number with that particular girl. I mean the one whose name was in the balloon he caught." This last Cindy hadn't seen, of course, but she had heard about it from one of the girls who had gone to the dance.

"What a clever idea!" Susan gazed at her admiringly. "We're thinking of using a St. Patrick's Day theme for the prom, but we might do the same thing using green balloons. It must have been fun."

"Yes." Cindy's tone was cold because she was feeling guilty again. Casting around in her mind for something else to talk about, she happened to glance at the clock on the wall behind the prescription counter. "Oh dear!" she cried with pretended dismay. "I don't mean to break this up but I really must start home this very minute. I have a dinner engagement this evening and I have to dress."

"A dinner engagement?" echoed Martha.

Cindy made her voice casual. "Yes, at Mack Gordon's."

Martha and Jan and Susan stared at her, visibly impressed. "Golly," breathed Susan. "You certainly work fast."

Cindy laughed lightly, in an amused, slightly superior way. "Oh, don't get the wrong idea. This is strictly a family affair." But her manner, as she spoke, belied her casual words.

The other three girls reacted accordingly. Susan said "Golly!" again and Jan said, somewhat wistfully, "I wish I knew your system."

Martha simply stared.

"Still, I didn't actually lie to them," Cindy told herself uneasily, after she'd said good-by to Martha and Jan and Susan at the corner. "I *do* have a dinner engagement at the Gordons' and it *is* strictly a family affair. So nobody could accuse me of being dishonest."

But her feeling of guilt persisted.

The dinner was to be at seven o'clock and it was only a few minutes past five when Cindy arrived home. Nevertheless, she went upstairs almost immediately and began to draw the water for her bath. For, as she reminded herself several times while she was undressing, this was an important night—perhaps the most important one in her life. If she could succeed in impress-

41

ing Mack Gordon this evening, her future in Wood-mont High School would be practically assured.

She spent twenty minutes trying to decide which dress to wear and finally chose her blue wool, not only because the magazine article had recommended blue for girls with her coloring, but also because she had read somewhere that blue was most boys' favorite color. And she took particular pains with her make-up, applying her lipstick with a brush as Margaret of the magazine article had been taught to do.

Even though she was fortified by the knowledge that she looked her best, Cindy was terribly nervous when the time came to leave, and she was so quiet during the drive to the other end of town, where the Gordons lived, that her father became concerned and wanted to know if she had something on her mind.

"Oh no," Cindy assured him shakily. "If I seem absent-minded, it's because I'm thinking about a physics test that's been scheduled for next week."

The Gordons' home was a rambling, two-story stone house at the end of a winding drive. Mr. and Mrs. Gordon met the Taylors at the door and they were so friendly and pleasant that, for a minute or two, Cindy relaxed in spite of herself. Then Mack wandered into the entrance hall and instantly she became as taut as a violin string. Instead of the slacks and sports jacket which were his usual school attire, Mack was wearing a gray flannel suit and he looked more handsome than ever.

Mrs. Gordon, a slender, gray-haired woman with eyes of the same brilliant turquoise as Mack's, introduced her son to Cindy's parents and then turned, smiling, to Cindy. "I understand you and Malcolm have already met."

"Yes." Cindy got a grip on herself and managed a weak smile in Mack's general direction.

"Hi." Mack's answering grin was careless. "How are you tonight?"

"Fine, thanks." With all her heart, Cindy wished that she could think of something more interesting to say. Luckily, however, their parents began to talk so there was no need for her to say anything more.

They went into the living room and, during the ensuing conversation, Cindy worked hard to control her quaking nerves. "Don't be an idiot," she scolded herself, sitting quietly beside her mother and doing her best to look composed and self-assured. "There's nothing to be nervous about even if it *is* Mack Gordon." But she didn't attempt to take part in the conversation because she was afraid to trust her voice, and she couldn't help feeling relieved when dinner was finally announced.

She managed to get through dinner, although her remarks for the most part were limited to "Please" and "Thank you." But at least she didn't upset her water glass or spill food on the tablecloth or do any of the other horrible things she had been afraid she might do. And then after dinner, when they returned to the living room, Mrs. Gordon suggested a game of bridge.

"But we don't want to bore you young people," she went on, smiling at Cindy. "Mack, why don't you play some of your records for Lucinda? She might enjoy hearing them."

Cindy would have preferred to stay close to the bridge table, where her silence wouldn't be so noticeable. Then, too, she was disturbed by the expression which flashed momentarily across Mack's face. It was a bored, resigned-looking expression which made her wonder suddenly if Mack weren't too happy about having to stay home and entertain the Taylors.

The expression was gone an instant later, however, and Mack's tone was polite as he said, "Sure thing! Come on, Cindy. We keep the record player in the family room."

"I must be imagining things," Cindy told herself, rising to follow him. "Anyway, I ought to be glad for a chance to be alone with him. How else can I hope to make an impression on him? I never see him alone at school and I don't dare put on an act in front of our families."

The family room turned out to be a large, informal one at the back of the house. In addition to the record player, it contained a radio, a television set, and an assortment of lamps, tables, and comfortable-looking chairs. Floor-to-ceiling shelves along one wall were crammed with books, Cindy noticed.

Mack saw her looking at the books and explained that one of his older brothers was fond of reading. "We call this a *family* room," he said, "but my brothers and I are the ones who use it most."

Cindy asked about his brothers and Mack said that he had two—both of them older and both in college.

"But they'll be home this summer," he added. "You'll probably meet them then."

"I hope so," Cindy thought fervently. "I hope we're such good friends by then that I'll be meeting them as a matter of course." Glancing around the room, searching for another topic of conversation, she noticed that the floor was covered with rubber tile, laid in an unusual design. "What a pretty floor!" she remarked. "I don't believe I've ever seen anything quite like it before."

"It's practical, anyhow," Mack returned carelessly. "Mother had it installed when we started dancing here —to save wear and tear on the parquet floor."

Cindy, who had begun to relax a bit, grew tense again at his words. Did he intend to dance tonight? And, if so, would she be able to follow him? She thought of the long-ago incident in Miss Regina Smith's dancing class, and Jimmy Albright's loud protest: "No, I won't dance with that old beanpole, Cindy Taylor . . . she walks all over our feet."

What if she were to walk all over Mack's feet?

He led her to the record player and motioned to some shelves on the wall behind it. "Well, there they are. Take your choice."

The shelves held dozens of record albums as well as

45

stacks of single records. Cindy glanced through some of the titles and saw that they represented a wide variety of music—everything from Brahms symphonies to the latest popular hits. She motioned hesitantly toward Brahms. "What about that? Brahms has always been one of my favorites."

Mack groaned. "Don't tell me you go for that long-hair stuff! My oldest brother does, too, but I get enough of it when he's home."

"Oh no," Cindy said quickly. Honesty compelled her to correct the misstatement and she amended, "Well—I mean I like it, but I like other kinds of music, too. All kinds, in fact. What would you like to hear?"

"What about some Dixieland jazz?" Mack pulled out one of the albums. "This is the genuine article. Wait'll you hear what Fats does to the trumpet solo."

"That sounds fine," Cindy murmured. Actually, Dixieland jazz was one kind of music about which she knew very little, but she was fairly certain that it was music intended for listening rather than dancing. And she was anxious to postpone dancing with Mack.

Mack piled several records on the player and turned it on. Taking a cushion from one of the chairs, he tossed it on the floor and indicated that it was for Cindy. A moment later, he sprawled beside her.

Side by side on the floor beside the record player, they listened to that album and to another. Luckily Mack wasn't reticent about airing his opinions, so it wasn't necessary for Cindy to say much, except to reply

46

to his comments. When she did, now and then, feel called upon to make a comment of her own, she did her best to sound informed, intelligent, and interested, and apparently her remarks satisfied Mack because he didn't take exception to any of them.

Then, when the last record ceased spinning, he suddenly got up, went to the shelves, and picked up two more records. "This is fun," he said, "but we ought to try a couple of dances before you go home." He put the records on the player and pulled Cindy to her feet. "Let's see how we get along."

To Cindy's dismay, the first dance number he had chosen was a fast one. And Mack, she soon discovered, was an expert dancer—even better than she had expected. At first he did only smooth, easy steps, so that, in spite of her nervousness, she was able to follow him. But then, as the first record ended and was followed by one with even faster tempo, he began to do more complicated steps and it became more and more difficult to keep up with him. She closed her eyes and gritted her teeth. "I can do it," she told herself. "All I have to do is concentrate."

She did concentrate and somehow she was able to get through the dance without stumbling or stepping on his feet or otherwise disgracing herself. The record ended and Cindy, exhausted but proud of herself, half expected Mack to say something complimentary—something about how well she danced or how much he had enjoyed dancing with her.

Mack, however, merely gave her one of his careless grins and said, "Not bad. We'll have to try it again sometime." And when he'd removed the records, he suggested that they return to the living room.

Cindy couldn't understand his indifference. Was he disappointed in her dancing, after all? Hadn't she followed him as adroitly as she'd thought?

It was only after they had rejoined their parents that she finally came up with what she thought was the right answer. Of course! That must be it. The reason Mack hadn't made any comment about her dancing was that he'd taken it for granted. A boy like Mack, handsome and self-assured, was probably accustomed to expert partners—had probably never danced with girls who *weren't* expert. Therefore, wasn't it only natural for him to take Cindy's dancing for granted? Didn't it prove that he had accepted her as the poised girl she was pretending to be?

"What it amounts to," Cindy thought, "is that I really made quite a lot of progress tonight. I can't expect someone like Mack to fall all over himself the very first time we're together. Didn't he say something about trying it again sometime? What more do I want?"

She would have been happier, though, if Mack had said something more definite about seeing her again.

CHAPTER

5

ON SUNDAY AFTERNOON, Cindy wrote her first letter to Sally:

It hardly seems possible that I've been here for more than a week already. It was pretty confusing at first, but I'm finally beginning to get everything and everybody straightened out. The teachers are swell and Miss Ferguson, my English teacher, is really super! She told me Friday that my first two themes had been *beautifully written*. Her very words, imagine! Of course, as you know, English always was my favorite subject. And the music supervisor, Miss Clarke, is darling, too. Oh yes, I've joined the Glee Club. Wouldn't you know?

Thinking about the Glee Club, Cindy put down her pen, got up from the maple desk which occupied one corner of her bedroom, and went to the window, where she stood for several minutes gazing at the yard. It had been snowing when she and her mother and father came out of church this morning and it had continued to snow steadily until about an hour ago. Now, however, the air was clear and a pale sun was peeping through the clouds, casting faint shadows on the soft white blanket which covered the lawn. Several children were tobogganing on a slope across the street and, watching them, Cindy was suddenly wistful. "If this were Exeter," she thought, "I'd be calling Sally and getting out my skis."

But here there was no Sally to call. Still, writing to her was the next best thing.

Returning to the desk, Cindy picked up her pen.

The kids here seem okay. And one of the boys in my class is terrifically good-looking. He's tall and blond and his name's Mack Gordon.

She paused again, frowning at the window. To her disappointment, the dinner last Wednesday at the Gordons' hadn't done a thing, as far as she could see, to improve her relationship with Mack. He was polite in a casual, remote way when they saw each other at school, but you couldn't, by any stretch of the imagination, say that he seemed *interested*. Maybe, under the circumstances, it would be better not to tell Sally too much about him.

50

Having decided this, she promptly did just the opposite:

As a matter of fact, we had dinner at Mack's house the other night. His father and mine work for the same company, which is how it all came about. After dinner, we listened to some records for a while and he asked me to dance. He's terribly sophisticated and all that, so you can imagine how I felt! I managed to get long okay, though, thanks to our practice sessions. But don't get any funny notions. He rates just about tops in Woodmont High and dates a lot of different girls, so I don't suppose I'll be seeing much of him. You know me, ha ha!

She paused once more, frowned, and added a hurried last paragraph.

Later on, when we're settled, I hope you'll be able to come for a visit. I'll let you know when it's okay. In the meantime, say hello to everybody for me, and don't forget to write—

Your pal,
Cindy

"And I *will* invite her down later on," Cindy thought, addressing an envelope and reaching for a stamp. "Once I've made the grade here and everybody is used to thinking of me as one of the popular girls, it won't matter if Sally does spill the beans about what I was like in Exeter. Because by then nobody will believe her.

51

But I don't dare risk it now. We'll both just have to be patient.

During the following days, Cindy found it necessary to remind herself frequently of the need for patience. She continued to dress carefully for school each day, taking particular pains with her nails and hair, and never wearing the same blouse or sweater twice in succession. She continued to "stand tall" and speak in a low voice. Nightly, standing before her mirror, she practiced the new and not yet familiar expressions which she had decided were appropriate to her role: a cool, poised smile to denote slightly bored amusement; a raised eyebrow to express casual interest; narrowed eyes and a haughty tilt of her head for those occasions when she didn't know what expression to use.

But there were times this week when she couldn't help wondering if she were making much headway. Martha and Jan and Susan, and some of their friends as well, seemed impressed; but none of the boys, including Mack, seemed to be paying any attention to her. And Rose Walsh was blandly indifferent, which worried Cindy considerably. It was important, she felt, to make an impression on Rose, because of her popularity with the boys.

She was reminded of Rose's importance once again on Wednesday afternoon after the Glee Club rehearsal. She was on her way to Weyman's Drugstore with Martha and Jan and Susan, and they had paused at a corner of Market Street to wait for the light to change, when Rose and Bill and Mack rode by in a station wagon. Mack was driving, and Martha explained that the station wagon belonged to his family.

"But the Gordons have two cars," Susan added, "so Mack has the use of the station wagon most of the time."

Rose was sitting between Mack and Bill, laughing up at Mack as they passed, and Cindy, pretending not to look, nevertheless noticed how confident Rose appeared. Raising one eyebrow to express casual interest, she said, "Rose is cetainly popular, isn't she?"

"Yes," said Martha with constraint, and there was a sudden odd silence like the one that had occurred before when Rose's name was mentioned. Then rather hurriedly, Cindy thought, her three companions began to talk of other things.

Cindy couldn't understand it. What was the cause of the other girls' peculiar attitude toward Rose? Was it possible, after all, that they were a little envious of her? Maybe one of them secretly liked Bill Norberry and they were jealous on that account.

Her mind was still on Rose when she and her companions took their places in one of the plastic and chrome booths. "Somehow," she thought, "I'm going to have to find out what's going on."

Her chance came a few moments later when the waitress brought their order, causing a lull in the conversation. Cindy took a sip of Coke and curved her lips in her new, poised smile. "By the way," she said, "there's something I've been meaning to ask you. I can't help noticing that you and most of the other girls are rather cool to Rose. She seems so attractive, I've been wondering what's wrong. I mean, don't you like her—or what?"

Martha and Jan and Susan exchanged a swift glance. Jan spoke first, addressing Martha and Susan in her quiet, slow-voiced way. "We might as well tell her. If we don't, somebody else will."

"Tell me?" Cindy said curiously. "Tell me what?"

"I suppose you're right." Martha looked distressed. "The truth is, Cindy, that Rose has the reputation of being a little wild."

Susan snorted. "A *little* wild, did you say?"

"Now, Sue, there's no need to exaggerate," Jan put in mildly.

"Who's exaggerating?" Susan tossed her head and eyed Jan belligerently. "You know as well as I do that she was kicked out of that girls' school last year!"

"Yes," Jan admitted, "but we don't know why."

"There must have been a good reason!" Susan muttered darkly. "Besides, that isn't all of it. You know yourself how she's always bragging about how late she stays out and all the night clubs she's gone to and—"

"I don't think we need go into that," Martha interrupted. She turned to Cindy. "I think we've answered your question about why we're not too friendly with Rose, haven't we?"

54

"Yes, you have," Cindy replied. Privately, however, she was far from satisfied with the explanation. The fact that Rose had been expelled from a private school was damaging but, on the other hand, everybody knew that girls' schools were usually pretty strict. Wasn't it possible, therefore, that Rose had committed only some minor indiscretion which had led to her expulsion? As for staying out late and going to night clubs, well, maybe Rose did these things and maybe she didn't. Maybe it was just a lot of talk.

Suddenly Cindy decided that she didn't want to hear any more. She stirred the ice in her Coke and took another sip. "By the way," she murmured, "have any of you ever been in the Gordons' house? They have a family room where Mack and his brothers hang out—and the floor is simply marvelous for dancing."

She knew, from the eager, interested way the other three girls looked at her, that she had succeeded in diverting their attention from Rose.

The two days following the Glee Club rehearsal were very much like the days which had preceded it. Cindy continued to dress meticulously, she continued to maintain her pose of unconcern, and she continued to practice her new expressions in front of her mirror each night. But nothing eventful happened until her second week in Woodmont was drawing to a close. And then Cindy's campaign received a big push forward from an unexpected source.

Late Friday afternoon, Miss Ferguson asked her to remain after school. Surprised and curious, Cindy waited at her desk while the class left by twos and threes and half dozens, most of them chattering about the new issue of the *Crimson Banner* which had come out that morning.

She didn't have to wait long. As soon as everyone had gone, Miss Ferguson put away the papers she had been correcting and motioned Cindy up to her desk. "Well, Lucinda," she said, "what do you think of the *Banner?* This is the first issue you've seen, isn't it?"

"Yes, it is," Cindy replied, "and I like it very much. It's a good paper."

"I'm glad you think so." Miss Ferguson smiled. "If you like it, I think you'll be interested in my suggestion. How would you like to be on the staff of the *Banner?*"

"B—be on the staff?" In her astonishment, Cindy stumbled over the words.

The teacher nodded. "As you may have suspected, I've been very favorably impressed by your work in English III. And I want to see talent like yours put to good use. So I mentioned you to the editor and showed him some of your work, and he said he'd be glad to have your help."

"The editor? Isn't that Peter Holmes?"

"Yes. Do you know Peter?"

"We've met." Cindy's excitement was mounting rapidly.

"So much the better," Miss Ferguson said. "Peter

didn't tell me, but if you and he already know each other, it should be that much easier for you to work together."

"But weren't the reporters all assigned a long time ago?"

"They were, but I'm not talking about a straight reporting job. What I have in mind for you is something more specialized. Sometimes the reporters fail to turn in their material on time; frequently a great deal of their material has to be rewritten. It all adds up to an extremely heavy load for the editor, and that's where you come in. What Peter needs is an assistant—someone who can handle some of the typing and rewriting and also write an occasional original story. I think you're right for the job and so does Peter. Would you like to try it?"

"Would I!" Cindy's heart was pounding, her pose forgotten. "When and where do I start?"

"The sooner the better," said Miss Ferguson. "Suppose I arrange with Peter to meet you here after school, Monday. We can go over the work in detail then, and give you your first assignment. Will Monday at four suit you?"

"I'll be here," Cindy said eagerly. "I'll be here with bells on!"

C H A P T E R

6

Aɴ ᴜɴꜱᴄʜᴇᴅᴜʟᴇᴅ ꜰᴀᴄᴜʟᴛʏ ᴍᴇᴇᴛɪɴɢ was called on Monday, necessitating a change in Miss Ferguson's plans.

"However, I'm sure you won't need me," she told Cindy. "Peter can tell you everything you need to know about your work on the *Banner*." She nodded to some departing students and glanced at her watch. "The meeting is scheduled for four-ten and it's five after now, so I'm afraid I'll have to leave you. But Peter should be along any minute."

Cindy said good-by and settled down at her desk to wait for Peter. Over the weekend, she'd lost none of her elation over her appointment to the staff of the newspaper; if anything, she was more excited than ever.

"But I'll have to be careful not to let Peter Holmes see how I feel," she reminded herself now, as the last of her classmates departed and the noise in the corridors began to dwindle. "He's probably pretty smart—he *must* be or he wouldn't be the editor of the paper. And if he sees how thrilled I am, he may suspect that nothing like this has ever happened to me before."

Trying to calm herself, she glanced around the room, noticing how different it looked when it was deserted. The freshly cleaned blackboard, with the erasers lined up beneath it, looked oddly bare and blank. And the long rows of desks had a rigid unfamiliarity. Unoccupied, they had lost their separate identities and become just what they were—lifeless pieces of furniture, made of wood and held together with metal bolts and bands. That one at the end of the second row was Mack Gordon's desk. It always seemed so special when Mack sat at it; how strange that it should look exactly like all the other desks now!

There was a sudden sound of footsteps in the corridor and, as Cindy looked up, Peter Holmes hurried through the door. He was wearing a gray poplin jacket over his sweater and carried a thick sheaf of papers under one arm. He saw Cindy and his face broke into a wide grin. "Hi, there, Cindy-short-for-Lucinda. Sorry I'm so late but I got tied up in a chemistry experiment in the lab and didn't get through till now."

Cindy flushed, wishing he would forget the Cindy-short-for-Lucinda" business. It sounded so kiddish. "It's quite all right," she murmured stiffly. "I'm in no hurry."

"Anyhow, as they say in the Navy, glad to have you

aboard." Peter glanced toward the teacher's desk. "Where's Miss Ferguson?"

"She had to leave for the teachers' meeting, but she said you'd tell me what to do."

"Okay." Peter strode across the room and perched on one corner of the desk opposite Cindy's. "I suppose she gave you the general idea, didn't she?"

"She said that it's mostly a matter of rewriting and typing, plus an occasional original story."

"That's it in a nutshell." Peter placed the sheaf of papers on Cindy's desk. Behind the shell-rimmed glasses, his brown eyes grew serious. "Right now, these are the most urgent. They're stories that have been turned in for the next issue of the *Banner*, and some of them will only need editing—changes in punctuation, corrections in spelling, and so forth. But some of them will have to be rewritten. Think you can handle it?"

Resisting her eagerness to look through the papers, Cindy gave them a single careless glance. "If you want me to."

Suddenly Peter frowned, drawing his dark eyebrows together until they were almost hidden behind the rims of his glasses. "Now look, if you don't want this job, say so. Miss Ferguson showed me some of your work and it was swell. But somehow I have the impression that you're not too keen about taking this thing on. If you aren't, the time to tell me is now."

Cindy realized that she'd overdone her pretended

indifference. "Of course I want the job," she said hastily.

"Okay." Peter surveyed her for a moment in silence, looking as though he didn't quite know whether to believe her or not. "I don't expect you to jump up and clap your hands. It's a hard job and, with the *Banner* coming out every other week, it takes a heck of a lot of time. That's why I need help." He glanced at the papers and frowned again. "One thing I should mention, though—if you come across any copy that's *too* illegible, skip it. Don't waste your time on anything that it would take a code expert to decipher. If the reporter was that lazy, his story doesn't deserve to get into print."

"I understand." Cindy picked up the papers and began to leaf through them, noticing that there were seven stories altogether.

"Now, about a typewriter—"

"We have a portable at home. It's my father's, but I know he won't mind my using it."

"Good." Peter's face cleared. "I was going to try to borrow one for you, but if you have one at home, so much the better. Be sure to triple space everything and . . . let's see . . . seems as though there was something else. Oh yes." He looked apologetic. "I hate to ask it, but do you think you could possibly manage to have these done by Friday?"

"I think so."

"Swell." Peter stood up and stretched to his full

61

height. "You don't know how much I appreciate this, Cindy. I'm so busy that I didn't see how I was ever going to have everything done in time. Later on I'd like you to write some original stuff, too, but for the next issue this is the most important job. It's really swell of you to help."

Cindy wondered what he would think if he knew that far from feeling imposed upon, she was having a hard time controlling her enthusiasm. Afraid that she might unconsciously betray her true feelings to Peter, she said almost indifferently, "It's no trouble."

Once more, Peter's glance was puzzled. "Well," he said after a moment, "I guess that about covers it for now. Any questions?"

"Where do you want me to meet you Friday?"

"Let's make it the school library, any time after four. There won't be any kids working there as exams are over. That's where I usually go when I have to work on the paper. The *Banner* office is too noisy—someone's always using the typewriter. Okay?"

"Okay."

Peter buttoned up his poplin jacket and pulled on his gloves, but he didn't make a move to go. "What are we waiting for?" he asked finally. "Aren't you going home?"

With a start, Cindy realized that he was waiting for her. "Yes, of course," she replied. "As soon as I get my coat."

On the way out, Peter told her that after high school

he planned to go to college and study journalism, and that he was hoping to enter the university in the nearby city. "So that I can come home over a weekend once in a while and visit my family," he explained.

Cindy asked about his family and he said that, in addition to his parents, he had a younger brother named Roy. "But you'd never know to look at us that we're related," Peter went on. "Roy's only thirteen but he's already an inch taller than I am. My dad's tall, too. I'm the runt of the family."

Something about his voice made Cindy wonder suddenly if Peter *minded* being of only average height. "You're not short," she said quickly. "Aren't you about five ten?"

"Five nine and a half."

"Well, that's certainly not what I'd call small."

"Now you sound like my mother. Oh well, I've long since resigned myself to the fact that I'll never be a six-footer." Peter's grin was philosophic. "And it has its compensations. For one thing, I never have to worry about ducking my head when I go through doorways." He gave her a sidelong glance. "There are times, though, when I wish I could add a few more inches."

Once again there had been something odd in his tone. Before Cindy could ask him what he meant, however, he began to talk about the *Banner,* and he continued to talk about the *Banner* until they parted.

That night Cindy took her father's portable typewriter to her room and went to work on her first assignment for the *Banner*. As Peter had indicated, the quality of the reporters' stories varied as much as the paper on which they were written. Some of them, like Martha Alexander's report of the last Home Economics Club meeting, were neat and concise and needed only minor corrections here and there. Others, however, were poorly written, and the poorest of all was Mack Gordon's report on the basketball team. A brief, penciled scrawl, obviously done in a hurry, it was almost useless. Reading it, Cindy was reminded of Peter's admonition not to waste time on illegible notes. But somehow she couldn't persuade herself to discard Mack's story.

"I'll save it for the last," she thought. "If I can get all the others done tonight, maybe I can dig up enough material about the team before Friday to fill in the gaps."

She worked late that night and managed to finish all of the stories except Mack's. The following day she went to the public library after school and got copies of the *Woodmont Daily Record* dating back to the opening of the Basketball season. Seated at a table in the reference room, she went through them one by one, taking copious notes whenever she found any news of the high school basketball team.

Wednesday was the day of the regularly scheduled glee club rehearsal and, after the rehearsal, Martha and Jan and Susan again invited Cindy to the drugstore with them. But on Thursday, she hurried home

64

after school and went to work immediately on the basketball story, filling in Mack's sketchy notes with the material she'd obtained at the library. By bedtime she was satisfied that she had made Mack's story one of the best.

She was a little late in leaving her last class Friday and when she reached the school library on the second floor, Peter was already there, working industriously at a long table near the window. He was in his shirt sleeves, with his poplin jacket folded over the back of a chair, and his dark hair looked rumpled, as though he'd been running his hands through it as he worked.

He looked up, smiling, as Cindy came through the door. "Hi, Cindy-short-for-Lucinda. How'd you get along with your first assignment?"

"All right, I think." Doing her best to look unconcerned, Cindy crossed the room and handed him the sheaf of neatly typewritten papers. "You be the judge."

"Okay, let's have a look." Motioning her to a chair beside him, Peter picked up her first story and began to read.

Cindy watched him silently, keeping her face expressionless because she didn't want him to see how much his approval meant to her. After a while she found herself thinking that, even though he wasn't handsome, there was something decidedly likable about Peter. She liked the quiet way he went about his work and she liked, too, the way one unruly lock of hair

65

kept falling over his forehead whenever he made the least motion, as when he turned a page.

He read on, going from one story to another without pause. At first it was impossible to tell what he was thinking, but presently he began to nod from time to time and, when he had finished the fourth story, he looked up and said, "Good work, Cindy!"

Before she could think of a word to say in reply, he had gone on to the next story.

Cindy had purposely placed the report of the basketball team at the bottom of the pile. As Peter began to read it, she edged forward anxiously, knowing that this was the most important story of all because it represented her best effort.

Peter was only about a third of the way through the report when he began to frown. He was still frowning when he came to the end and looked up again.

There was a long silence. "What's wrong?" Cindy asked. "Don't you like it?"

"There's nothing wrong with the story. It's swell, in fact. But it isn't Mack Gordon's work."

"Oh, but it is! I wrote it from his notes. All I did was add a little here and there to dress it up, sort of."

Peter shook his head and the dark lock of hair tumbled over his forehead again. He brushed it back absently. "I know better. I *saw* Mack's notes and very nearly threw them away. Only gave them to you because I thought you might be able to salvage one or

66

two paragraphs we could use as a filler. The last thing I expected was a complete report like this."

"Then you aren't going to use it?" Cindy tried hard not to show her disappointment.

"I didn't say that. I'm going to use it because it's too good to keep out. But I think it ought to go in under your by-line."

"Oh no!" In her dismay, Cindy forgot her resolution to remain calm on the surface no matter what happened. She gripped the edge of the table. "Please don't do that! I'd rather you didn't print it at all than give me the credit! Won't you please put it in under Mack's name?"

"If you aren't a funny one!" Peter's expression was a combination of surprise and bewilderment. "Just about the time I think you don't give a darn about anything, you turn around and—" He broke off, shaking his head. "But if it means that much to you, okay. In it goes—under Gordon's by-line." He grinned wryly. "Bet Mack'll be surprised when he reads it."

"And pleased, too, I hope," Cindy thought to herself. She settled back in her chair and, with an effort, managed to regain some of her poise. "What about the other stories? Are they all right? What I mean is, do I get the job?"

"For as long as you want it," Peter replied. "I knew from the samples Miss Ferguson showed me that you could write. But these," he gestured toward the stories, "are even better than I expected. Obviously you've put

67

a lot of time and thought into them. So much, in fact, that I—" Again he broke off, shaking his head and eying her as though something about her puzzled him.

Cindy squirmed self-consciously. Had she been too conscientious about her work? Was Peter beginning to suspect that she was naturally the diligent type?

Suddenly he grinned. "Well, never mind. They say that time provides the answer to all things." Shoving back his chair, he began to gather up the books and papers scattered on the table. "That about winds it up for this week, Cindy, as far as the *Banner* is concerned. But say—" He hesitated and his cheeks reddened slightly. "I have an idea. If you're not doing anything tomorrow night, what about the two of us taking in a movie? Or better yet, if I can get Dad's car, we might take a run out to Gorley's."

It was Cindy's turn to hesitate. Surprised, she was torn between two desires. She'd heard about Gorley's, a restaurant which had a small dance floor and was located about five miles from town on the most direct highway to the city. Martha and the other girls had told her that it was a favorite dating spot of the Woodmont High students. The thought of going there with Peter was almost overwhelmingly tempting. But what would Peter think of her if she accepted his very first invitation—and for the very next night, at that? Wouldn't it be better in the long run—and far more in keeping with her new role—if she played hard-to-get?

She hesitated for an instant longer and made up her

mind. "I'm sorry, Peter," she said carefully, "but I'm afraid I can't make it tomorrow night. I have another engagement."

"Oh." It was hard to tell from Peter's expression whether or not he was disappointed. "Guess I'll have to take a rain check then."

"I guess so," Cindy said uneasily. Now that she'd declined his invitation, she half regretted her decision. What if he weren't interested enough to ask her again?

C H A P T E R

7

CONSIDERING THE FACT that she had been there only three weeks, Cindy thought she had really done quite well.

It was the Tuesday afternoon following her talk with Peter, and once again she was in the study hall in Room 304. She had finished her French assignment five minutes earlier, and was sitting idly at her desk, waiting for the final bell, and thinking about all that had taken place since her arrival in Woodmont. And, as she had just reassured herself, it seemed to her that she had made substantial progress in some respects. She was doing well in her studies, she had joined the Glee Club, and she had been appointed to the staff of the *Banner*. And, by working hard at her sophisticated pose, she had managed to impress some of her new classmates. At least Martha, Jan, and Susan and their circle of friends seemed to be convinced that she had led a gay and glamorous life in Exeter. Apparently she'd succeeded in interesting Peter Holmes, too, since he'd asked her for a date.

In other ways, however, Cindy had to admit that she wasn't entirely satisfied with her accomplishments. Some of her classmates, like Mack Gordon and Rose Walsh and Bill Norberry, still seemed almost unaware of her presence in Woodmont High. And even Martha and Jan and Susan, now that Cindy stopped to think of it, could hardly be called close friends. Occasionally one or another of them would invite her downtown after school or walk part way home with her, but none of them ever telephoned her and she'd never been invited to any of their homes. Certainly she had no one in Woodmont who could be described as the kind of friend that Sally Baird had been in Exeter.

Thinking of Sally, Cindy felt the familiar, recurring stab of guilt. There had been a letter from Sally in this morning's mail. She had read it during her lunch hour and had been feeling uncomfortable about it ever since. Sally's letter was full of news about Exeter, but she also made it clear that she was lonely, eager to visit Cindy in Woodmont:

Just let me know when it suits you. Mother and Dad said that if they couldn't drive me down, they'd put me on a train or bus. I've been moping around the house so much since you've been gone, I think they'll be glad to get rid of me for a couple of days!

"And I want to see Sally, too," Cindy thought for the hundredth time since noon. "There's nothing I'd like better than to sit down with her and have a good long talk, the way we used to do. But I can't invite her yet— not until I've made the grade here. In the long run, Sally will enjoy the visit more, too, if I wait until I have lots of friends. I'll be able to show her a *much* better time."

The bell rang, signaling the end of the period, and, as usual, Cindy rose quickly, holding her head high, and hurried toward the door, trying to look as though she had an immediate and important engagement. She had taken perhaps half a dozen steps when she felt a light touch on her shoulder and, turning, found herself face to face with Rose Walsh.

Rose, beautiful as ever in a red sweater which matched her lipstick, was smiling. "What's the hurry?" she asked. "Going anywhere in particular?"

Cindy gulped. It was the first time that Rose had made an overture. "Why, no, I don't have anything special in mind. Why?"

Rose's shrug was indifferent. "Oh, I thought if you weren't doing anything, we might walk down to Weyman's."

"Suits me." Cindy did her best to copy the dark-haired girl's nonchalance. But she was surprised and elated. Rose didn't bother much with other girls, so the fact that she had noticed Cindy was significant.

And Rose dated Bill, who was Mack's best friend. What if Mack and Bill happened to come into Weyman's while Cindy was there with Rose? What if today should mark the beginning of something *important?*

All of this ran through Cindy's mind while she and Rose returned to their home room and put away their books. They went to the locker room to get their coats, and Rose stayed at Cindy's side, chattering about trivialities as though there were nothing at all unusual about her sudden invitation.

They were outside and starting down the steps when she said abruptly, "What's this I hear about your being on the staff of the *Banner*, Cindy? Is it true?"

"Yes, I started last week," Cindy answered proudly. "They made me a sort of special assistant to Peter Holmes."

"Nice going." Rose gave her a knowing glance. "You must have pulled quite a few strings to land a prominent position like that."

"As matter of fact, I—" On the verge of telling Rose how the appointment had come about, Cindy checked herself. It had suddenly occurred to her that Rose wasn't the sort to be impressed by scholarship. "It wasn't so hard," she finished awkwardly.

Rose laughed with obvious disbelief. "All right, be mysterious if you like."

Several boys were standing across the street from

the school, and Cindy saw that one of them was Peter Holmes. She caught his eye and waved, and Peter grinned and waved in return. His glance settled on Rose and he looked a little surprised, Cindy thought.

The two girls turned the corner. "How do you like working with Peter?" Rose asked casually.

"Oh, fine," Cindy replied. "He asked me for a date last Saturday."

"Really?" Rose's tone was only mildly interested. "How was it?"

"I didn't go. I—I had another engagement."

"Oh." Rose glanced at Cindy speculatively. "One of your old Exeter boy friends, I suppose. I hear you dated a number of different boys there. One of them was the senior class president, they say."

"Oh, Bob Evans," Cindy murmured self-consciously, marveling at the powers of the grapevine. She wondered how much rumor had to do with Rose's sudden interest in her. Quite a bit, she guessed. Rose wasn't the kind to go out of her way for a nobody.

Trying to live up to Rose's apparent conception of her, she said, "You'd like Bob, I think. He's awfully good-looking and a terrific dancer."

"Really?" Rose sounded definitely interested now. "How would you say he compares with Peter Holmes, for instance?"

"With Peter?" Cindy hesitated, wondering how to answer when she actually didn't know much about either boy. She chose her words carefully. "I'd say they

74

were completely different types. Peter's far more serious than—than most of the boys I knew in Exeter."

To her surprise, Rose began to laugh. "So that's why you turned him down!" Linking her arm through Cindy's, she lowered her voice confidentially. "Frankly, that's my opinion, too. I've never dated Peter, but I can't imagine he'd be much fun. Personally I prefer smoother, more sophisticated boys like Bill and Mack, don't you?"

"Oh yes!" Cindy agreed, and immediately felt a little disloyal to Peter. "But it's true," she thought to herself. "Even though I like Peter, I do like Mack better."

Eager to enhance her new standing with Rose, she went on, "I've never danced with Bill, of course, but I think Mack's a rather nice dancer."

"I didn't know you had dated Mack." Rose's voice was suddenly suspicious.

Realizing her error, Cindy hastened to explain about the dinner at the Gordons' home. "So you see," she concluded, "it wasn't a date. Just one of those dull family affairs—and Mack was probably as bored as I was."

The explanation seemed to satisfy Rose. "Oh, I don't know," she said graciously. "Maybe he enjoyed it more than you think."

"And let that be a lesson to me," Cindy thought, as they entered the drugstore. Rose gets around and probably knows exactly who's dating whom. Next time

I'd better stop and think before I start dropping names."

In the drugstore, Cindy glanced around quickly, hoping to see Bill and Mack, but Weyman's was deserted except for the employees and two older men who were standing near the cigar counter. The girls sat in one of the booths, and at first Cindy kept looking up every time she heard the door open. But none of the high school crowd came in, and presently Rose said that Bill had stayed after school to make up an exam. "As for Mack," she added, "Heaven only knows where he is. Probably riding around in his station wagon."

"Probably," Cindy agreed nervously. Now that she and Rose had ordered their Cokes, she was wondering what she could possibly find to talk about that would impress Rose.

As it turned out, she needn't have worried, because Rose did most of the talking. She spoke of her dates with Bill and other boys, including some college boys whom she said she dated now and then when they were home for weekends. She talked about where she had gone on some of her dates, describing various night clubs around town in enough detail to prove that she was familiar with them. Sitting quietly across from her, Cindy tried hard to pretend that she, too, was accustomed to such places, but she couldn't help feeling out of her depth. And the longer she listened, the more uncomfortable she grew. There was something so wise, so knowing, about Rose—a genuine sophistication that

76

made Cindy's pretended poise seem feeble and pale by comparison.

"I'll never be like that *really*," Cindy thought, listening with concealed amazement to the smooth flow of talk from the other side of the table. "I've never had anything like her experience and I never will. And I'll never, never be able to achieve that superior air of hers."

But Cindy must have been doing better than she thought for, as they were leaving, Rose said, "This has been fun, Cindy. It's been a long time since I've run into anybody who feels the way I do about things. We'll have to get together again soon."

Cindy glanced at the other girl quickly. Had Rose guessed the truth? Was she making fun of her?

But Rose's eyes were innocent of guile. Apparently she meant what she said and really believed that she and Cindy were two of a kind.

It was three days before Cindy talked with Rose again, and in the meantime she had a rather odd conversation with Peter. It took place early Wednesday afternoon when she and Peter happened to return from lunch at the same time and met at the entrance to the school.

"Don't forget to pick up your copy of the *Banner* Friday," Peter said, holding the door open for her.

"I won't forget," Cindy assured him.

They started down the corridor and Peter grinned at

her mischievously. "If you look hard enough, you may come across your name somewhere in this issue."

Cindy halted, dismayed. "Peter, you didn't—"

"No." His grin widened. "I gave Gordon the by-line on the basketball story. But if I were you, I'd pay particular attention to the box on the editorial page, listing the names of the staff."

"Oh." Cindy's smile was a mixture of relief and anticipation. She hadn't expected her name to appear on the staff list so soon.

They walked down the corridor. "I see you've been getting acquainted with some of your classmates," Peter said.

Cindy nodded absently, her mind still on the *Banner*. There was a short pause.

"You're new here," Peter went on then, half as though speaking to himself, "and you probably haven't made up your mind about most of the kids yet." His face was expressionless but his voice was odd—so odd that it bothered Cindy. Something about it reminded her of the way Martha and the other girls sounded when they spoke of Rose.

They reached the door of her room and halted again. "Any more work for me to do for the *Banner*?" she asked.

"Not yet," said Peter. "If you'll stop in at the library after school on Friday, though, I'll probably have some more rewrites for you."

"I'll be there," Cindy promised.

They said good-by then and she went into the room. Every now and then that afternoon, however, her mind returned to the conversation with Peter, and she couldn't help wondering about the peculiar way he'd spoken.

The rest of the week was uneventful until Friday, when the new issue of the *Banner* came out. Remembering what Peter had said, Cindy turned at once to the editorial page and she felt a quick thrill of pride when she saw "Lucinda Taylor" listed as a member of the staff. She was proud, too, of her rewrites; most of them read much better in print than they had in manuscript, she thought. And the best of all was Mack's basketball team story. Would Mack notice it? she wondered. And, if so, would he try to find out who had done so much work on it?

Several people saw Cindy's name in the paper that morning and congratulated her, but Mack wasn't one of them. However, late in the morning, something happened which drove all thoughts of the *Banner* from Cindy's mind.

She was on her way to physics class when Rose strolled up to her. "Hi," she said carelessly. "I see it's now official that you're a member of the *Banner* staff. As I said before, nice going!"

"Thanks." Cindy tried to sound casual.

"Which reminds me," Rose continued. "There's something I want to ask you."

"Oh?"

"The idea came to me after we were downtown the other day. Why don't we get together and have a double date soon?"

"Why—why, that would be nice." Cindy did her best to conceal her surprise.

"I think so." Rose nodded and shot Cindy a quick, questioning glance. "What about tomorrow night? I have a date with Bill. Are any of your Exeter boy friends coming down?"

Cindy swallowed. "No, I—uh—decided to stay home tomorrow night and get caught up on some other things."

"Oh." Rose looked disappointed. "Couldn't you change your mind?"

"I could, I guess." Cindy swallowed again. "But it would be too late to get in touch with any of the Exeter boys now."

"I suppose so." Rose gazed at her thoughtfully. "I could get you a date here, if you want me to."

"It might be fun." Cindy's grip on her physics textbook tightened involuntarily.

"Let me see, who could we—?" Rose paused, frowning. Suddenly she snapped her fingers. "What about Mack Gordon? If he doesn't have a date, I think I could get him."

"Mack Gordon?" Cindy's voice almost squeaked in spite of her efforts to control it. "Why, yes, Mack would be okay."

"All right, I'll see what I can do. I'll let you know if

Mack can't make it. Otherwise, you'll be hearing from him."

Rose left her, and Cindy went on to her class. But she was almost dizzy with excitement and she was still up in the clouds when she went home for lunch at noon. She couldn't eat much, although her mother had prepared vegetable soup and the molded salad that was her favorite.

"I'm going to have a date with Mack Gordon. I'm going to have a date with Mack Gordon!" Cindy's mind was so preoccupied with the dazzling thought that afternoon that she almost forgot to go to the library at four. She remembered her appointment with Peter just as she was leaving the building, and retraced her steps to the second floor, where she found Peter hard at work at the long table.

"Find your name in the paper this morning?" he asked, grinning at her as she came through the door.

"Yes, thanks." Cindy returned his grin and went over to the table. She glanced at the papers strewn over its top. "Any rewrites for me!"

"Not yet." Peter explained that most of the papers contained material for an editorial he was writing. "However, I think we're going to need a filler next time," he said. "Something original, about five hundred words. Think you could write something and have it ready by the middle of next week?"

"Fiction or nonfiction?"

"Either one. It's up to you."

"Yes, I can do it." She'd probably spend most of tomorrow getting ready for her date with Mack, Cindy was thinking, but five hundred words wasn't much. She could probably write the whole thing Sunday afternoon. She smiled hazily at Peter. "Anything else?"

"No, that's all for now." Peter's brown eyes crinkled at the corners. "Unless you'll let me come up tomorrow night for that date you wouldn't give me last week?"

Cindy shook her head. "Sorry, but I'm afraid I'm tied up again."

"Well, never let it be said that I don't keep trying," Peter remarked cheerfully.

He was, Cindy thought, almost *too* cheerful about it —as though he didn't really care whether she was busy or not. A trifle hurt, she made short work of saying good-by.

CHAPTER

8

IT SEEMED to Cindy that the telephone had never been so silent as it was on Saturday. She hovered around it most of the morning, reminding herself frequently that even if it did ring the call might be from Rose, saying that she hadn't been able to get Mack. But always, in the back of Cindy's mind, there was the thought that the caller might be Mack himself.

The few calls which came that morning, however, were all for her mother.

Nevertheless, Cindy went ahead with preparations for the possible double date. After lunch she washed and dried her hair, brushing it until it shone like silk, and she gave herself a manicure, using the new polish she'd bought on the way home from school yesterday. The problem of what to wear was difficult, but she finally decided on her blue wool. Even though Mack had seen it before, it was her most becoming dress and would, she thought, be suitable for almost any. place they happened to go.

She had explained carefully to her parents that the date was not yet definite. "It depends on whether or not Mack's free," she'd said, thankful that they already knew Mack so she didn't have to answer a lot of questions about him. "Rose just had this idea on the spur of the moment and it's pretty short notice, so perhaps he'll be busy with something else."

"I don't know, Cindy," her father said. "It seems to me that if young Gordon wanted to—"

"Now, Henry, you're forgetting that Lucinda's still a comparative stranger here," her mother interrupted. She smiled at Cindy. "I think it will be all right, since we know Mack and his family. Just make certain that you'll be home by twelve."

"I won't forget," Cindy promised, grateful for her mother's understanding.

"But I'd better not say anything to Rose and Bill and Mack about having to be in by twelve," she thought now, as she examined the blue wool dress to see if it needed to be pressed. They might think a midnight curfew was sort of childish.

As the afternoon wore on, however, Cindy began to worry less and less about being in by twelve and more and more about whether she'd go out at all. Her mother and father went to do the marketing in the middle of the afternoon and were gone for nearly two hours;

84

when they returned Cindy had not yet heard from either Rose or Mack. Nor did she receive a call during dinner.

By seven o'clock she had almost given up hope. "Rose," she told herself, "must have discovered that Mack had another date." Or perhaps Rose had changed her mind and hadn't asked him. Either way, she should have called, of course, but she probably hadn't realized how much Cindy was counting on the date.

"But I wish I hadn't told Mother and Dad about it until I knew for sure," Cindy thought. "They're trying to act as though they don't know what's going on, but they do know—and that makes it all the more embarrassing."

And then, just as she was starting to look through the newspapers to see what shows would be on television that evening, the phone rang and, when she answered, it was Mack.

"I understand we're stepping out tonight," he said nonchalantly.

A wave of relief swept over Cindy. "Why, yes, I guess we are."

"How about my coming up for you in about an hour? I can drop Bill off at Rose's on the way and we'll pick them up later."

"In an hour?" Cindy pretended to hesitate. "Why, yes, I think I can make it."

"Okay, you can look for me around eight, then," said Mack.

Cindy returned to the living room. "That was Mack," she announced, doing her best to sound calm. "I guess we're having that date with Rose and Bill, after all. He'll be here in an hour."

"Oh?" Her mother's voice was similarly offhand. "Anything I can do to help?"

"No, thanks," Cindy replied. She flew upstairs and, for the next hour, all was rush and confusion in her bedroom. In spite of the fact that she'd made such extensive preparations for the date earlier, she was so nervous that one minor catastrophe after another occurred. First she upset a box of powder and then she accidentally scraped the polish off one nail and had to redo it. She combed and rearranged her hair three times before she was finally satisfied with it.

When Mack arrived, shortly after eight, she purposely waited in her room for a few minutes so that she wouldn't seem too eager, and then she walked slowly downstairs.

Mack, perfectly at ease and handsome in gray flannel, was talking with her mother and father. He rose as Cindy came into the room. "Hi! How nice you look tonight!"

Something about the way he made the remark caused Cindy to wonder suddenly if it was his stock greeting to all of his dates. But she murmured "Thank you" and mentally thanked her lucky stars that she had managed not to blush.

They talked for a while with her parents, then Mack

said easily, "Well, if you're ready, I think we'd better get started. We don't want to keep Rose and Bill waiting." He helped Cindy into her coat, there was a brief flurry of good-byes, and they were on their way.

Cindy had rehearsed a number of clever, amusing things to say to Mack, but once she was alone with him in the station wagon she was too self-conscious to say anything. And Mack, too, was quiet, driving along the dark streets with a preoccupied air as though his mind were a thousand miles away. They were within a block of Rose's house when he said suddenly, "I understand you're responsible for my scintillating story in yesterday's *Banner*."

Cindy caught her breath. "Who told you?"

"Holmes." Mack laughed carelessly. "I'd never have known it was my story." It was the last thing he said until they reached Rose's house.

"Where will it be?" Rose asked, as she and Bill climbed into the back seat. "Anybody have any ideas?"

"What about the Hi-Ho Club?" Bill suggested.

Rose groaned. "Not again! I'm sick to death of that place. I'd rather go to the Terrace Room."

"That's where we went last week," said Bill.

"Well, does anyone have a better idea?" Rose said petulantly.

Cindy decided that it was time to show them that she knew her way around, too. "Why don't we go to Gorley's?"

The silence in the station wagon was sudden and complete.

Mack spoke first. *"Gorley's?"*

Cindy bit her lip, wondering what she had said that was wrong. Hadn't Martha and Jan and Susan told her that Gorley's was a favorite dating spot?

"Have you ever been there?" Bill wanted to know.

"No, but I've heard that it's very nice," Cindy replied uncertainly.

Rose giggled. "You know, it *might* be fun for a change. It's so long since we've been there at least it would be a novelty."

"Okay, if you insist." Mack shrugged and turned on the ignition. But, as he nosed the station wagon away from the curb and headed toward the highway, he again lapsed into a preoccupied silence. He didn't speak during the five-mile drive to Gorley's, in spite of Cindy's somewhat desperate attempts to draw him out.

Gorley's restaurant was a weather-beaten building several yards back from the highway and surrounded by a wide, graveled parking lot. As Mack pulled into an empty space at the rear of the lot, Cindy noticed that a number of cars were parked, and the sight reassured her. "Even if Mack isn't too happy about coming here," she thought, "he'll probably feel better when he sees some of the other kids."

The interior was divided into two rooms. The lunch counter, soda fountain, and cash register were in the small front room; beyond them, a latticed archway, painted a bilious green, led into a larger room which was evidently the main dining room and dance hall. Cindy, with Mack at her elbow, followed Rose and Bill past the lunch counter and through the archway, and then she halted, catching her breath in surprise. Although the main room was more than half-filled, there wasn't a person whom she recognized. There was a group of younger boys and girls sitting together at a table on one side of the dance floor, but the other customers were all in their twenties and thirties, most of them with the settled look of married couples.

A waitress came up and led Cindy and her companions to a table diagonally across the floor. As soon as she had taken their order, Rose turned to Cindy and smiled superiorly. "Well, what do you think of the place?"

Cindy looked around the room in bewilderment. "Where is everybody? I expected to see some of the other high school kids here."

"So that's it!" Rose laughed and slipped out of her coat, tossing it carelessly over the back of her chair. She was wearing a soft woolen dress in winter white which emphasized her vivid coloring. "Someone's been misleading you, Cindy."

"You mean the high school crowd doesn't come here?"

"Some of them do." Rose glanced significantly at Bill and Mack. "But we outgrew this place a long time ago."

"But where are they tonight?" Cindy persisted. "I mean the ones who do come here."

"Your guess is as good as mine." Rose's tone was indifferent. "Probably at the Rec."

"The wreck?"

"Rose means the Recreation Center in the park," Bill explained. "They have a Teen-Hi night there once a month and this happens to be the night. Didn't anybody tell you?"

"No, they didn't." Cindy wondered why Martha and Jan and Susan hadn't mentioned it to her.

"Don't let it worry you." Rose laughed disdainfully. "Those Teen-Hi affairs are ghastly dull. You wouldn't like them."

"What do they do for entertainment? Dance?"

"If you could call it that. Most of the time they play dumb games like twenty questions. Kid stuff! I wouldn't be caught dead at one of those things."

"Same here." Mack lit a cigarette and blew smoke out lazily. For the first time since entering Gorley's, he looked directly at Cindy. "You aren't one of those persons who enjoys parlor games, are you?"

"Oh, no!" Cindy replied quickly, hoping that her face hadn't given her away.

Bill turned to Mack. "Say, before I forget it, Mack, that was quite a story you had in the *Banner* yesterday. I didn't know you could write like that!"

"Neither did I," Rose said admiringly.

"You underestimate me." Mack looked complacent. "I'm a man of many and varied talents!"

Cindy stared at him in surprise. Wasn't he going to tell them about the part *she* had played in writing the story?

Obviously he wasn't. He was talking with Bill about the basketball team.

"But why should he say anything about me?" Cindy asked herself hurriedly. "After all, I'm the one who insisted on his having the by-line. Besides, I'm sure it wasn't an *intentional* oversight. Talking about the story made him think of the team and he simply *forgot* to mention me."

Mack and Bill continued to talk about the team until Rose pushed back her chair. "Since we're here, we might as well see if they have any decent records," she said restlessly. "Coming, Bill?"

Bill followed her across the floor to the jukebox and, a few moments later, a dance tune with a quick tempo filled the air, and Rose and Bill were dancing. Presently they were joined on the dance floor by three or four of the older couples.

For a while, Mack and Cindy watched them in silence. Then, as the first record ended and a second one began, Mack turned to Cindy. "Care to dance?"

"I don't mind." Cindy tried to sound as indifferent as he did.

"Come on, then." Mack crushed out his cigarette. "Nothing else to do in this dump."

And so, a moment later, Cindy once again found herself in his arms. As before he did complicated steps, but this time Cindy found him a little easier to follow. "It's because I have a better idea of what to expect," she thought, encouraged. "If we keep on having dates and I keep on dancing with him, the time may come when I won't even be nervous."

After the dance with Mack she danced once with Bill while Mack danced with Rose, and when they returned to their table, the waitress had brought their order.

Mack scowled with obvious distaste at the sandwich and Coke he had ordered. "Big deal!" he muttered.

Rose laughed lightly. "Might as well make the best of it, Mack. This isn't the Hi-Ho Club, you know."

"Don't I know it!" Mack took a sip of his Coke and grimaced. "But it'll be a long time before anybody talks me into coming to this dump again."

"We wouldn't think of trying." Rose smiled knowingly at Cindy. "Now that you've seen what it's like, you won't want to come here again, will you?"

"Oh no," said Cindy. Secretly, however, she couldn't understand her companions' scorn of Gorley's. The food was good, the dance floor was smooth, and the other customers, even though they were mostly older, seemed to be pleasant, well-behaved people.

"But they probably don't really mean it," she thought, gazing uneasily at Rose and the two boys. "Chances are, it's only their way of talking, and I won't think anything of it, once I'm used to them."

As the evening passed, however, she continued to feel ill at ease. She danced twice more with Mack and once again with Bill, and managed to follow both boys without stumbling or stepping on their feet. But between dances, when they all sat at the table talking, she found the going more difcult. She had never been very good at small talk and it was harder than ever when so many of the things the other three talked about—places they had seen, people they had known, and experiences they had shared—were unfamiliar to her. Then, too, she couldn't help noticing that both Bill and Mack seemed to be paying far more attention to Rose than they were to her.

"But that's only natural," she told herself repeatedly. "After all, they've known Rose much longer than they've known me. The important thing is that I *am* here with Mack and I'm dancing with him and getting acquainted with him. Which is certainly far more exciting than anything I ever did in Exeter."

If only she didn't feel so much like a fifth wheel!

It was just a few minutes after eleven when Mack suggested leaving. "That is, if everybody's had enough of this," he added.

"I have," said Rose.

"Same here," Bill agreed.

Mack looked at Cindy. "Think you can tear yourself away from this exhilarating atmosphere?"

"Any time you say." She pretended to yawn.

The boys called for the check and, a few minutes

93

later, they were outside and once again clambering into the station wagon. Conscious of her curfew, Cindy was afraid that the other three intended to go on to some other night spot, but she relaxed momentarily when Mack headed the car back toward Woodmont. Presently, however, she began to worry again because of his silence. What was he thinking? Was he bored with her, as well as with Gorley's? Would he tell Rose privately never to stick him again with a dull, uninteresting date like Cindy Taylor?

Why couldn't she think of something to say to him? Why couldn't she be like Rose, who didn't seem to be having a bit of trouble finding things to talk about with Bill?

The station wagon was in the outskirts of Woodmont when Rose happened to mention the junior prom.

Mack's head turned slightly. "That's right, it's next month, isn't it?" he said over his shoulder.

"March eighth," answered Bill. "You planning on going?"

"I don't know." Mack was silent for a moment. "I haven't made up my mind yet."

It was all that he said but, as he drove on, Cindy's heart did a sudden leap. Was he thinking of inviting *her?*

The thought that he might even be considering such a thing went a long way toward making up for an evening which had not quite come up to her expectations.

CHAPTER

9

MACK GORDON—His name was on Cindy's lips when she fell asleep Saturday night and when she awoke again the next moning. *Mack Gordon*—She continued to think about him all morning, during breakfast and afterward, when she went to church with her mother and father. At times it hardly seemed possible that she'd actually had a date with him, had driven out to Gorley's with him, and had danced with him—not once but several times.

At other times, however, the events of the night before were vivid in Cindy's mind and, even in retrospect, she had to admit that Mack hadn't exactly showered her with attention.

Mack Gordon was still very much in her thoughts that afternoon when she sat down at her desk to write the original story Peter had asked her to do for the

Banner. It was hard to shake her mind free of Mack and concentrate on the task at hand.

This, if accepted, would be Cindy's first by-line story in the school paper and she felt that it had to be good—good enough to make Mack and everyone else in Woodmont High sit up and take notice. At the same time, it had to be in keeping with her new personality, which automatically ruled out a great many subjects about which she could have written.

After discarding at least half a dozen ideas as being either too serious or too commonplace, she finally hit upon an idea which she thought might fill the bill. Why not write a satire about correct telephone usage? She could do it in the style of those articles the telephone company was always mailing to its subscribers, but with the advice deliberately reversed and—

Inserting some paper in the typewriter, she knit her brows in concentration for a few minutes and began to type:

First of all, never identify yourself to a telephone caller if you can avoid doing so. Keep him guessing as long as possible and, if he does the same thing, you'll both be able to prolong the call and postpone the moment when you have to hang up and start on your homework. If you must reveal your identity, get into a comfortable position without delay so that no unnecessary strain will be placed on your heart or brain. Some people prefer to lie on the floor, with their feet propped on the nearest chair, while others . . .

She wrote on and on, pausing occasionally to read over what she had written and to cross out a word or a sentence. It was late afternoon by the time she came to the last paragraph. She wrote after a moment's thought:

Remember, if all else fails and you run out of things to say to each other, you and your caller can always hang up, think about your conversation for five minutes, and call each other back again. By then, you should be good for at least another half hour.

She unrolled the last sheet of paper, read the story through, and nodded. It was the right length and it ought to attract plenty of attention. Furthermore it was almost bound to give the impression that Lucinda Taylor was the kind of girl who received many telephone calls. She was well satisfied with her afternoon's work.

But when she showed the story to Peter the next day, his reaction surprised her. Seated at the long library table, with his brown hair tumbling over his forehead, Peter chuckled several times while reading the story, but when he looked up again his eyes were a trifle disappointed.

"What's wrong?" she asked anxiously. "Don't you like it?"

"It's clever," he replied slowly. "To be completely honest about it, though, it's not quite what I expected from you."

Cindy stared at him. "What do you mean?"

97

"I don't know. I guess I was expecting something with more—depth." Peter frowned thoughtfully at the manuscript. All at once his face cleared and he placed the story on a small pile at the end of the table. "But never mind, we have room for stories like this, too. I imagine most of the kids will get a big kick out of it."

"Then you're going to use it?"

"Sure. Never said I wouldn't. I may save it for the issue after next, though. We're getting more material for the March first issue than I'd figured on." Peter leaned back in his chair and, behind the shell-rimmed glasses, his eyes took on an odd, almost shy look. "I was surprised not to see you at the Rec, Saturday night," he said abruptly. "When you said you had a date, I sort of took it for granted you'd be there."

"Oh." Cindy gazed with pretended nonchalance at her charm bracelet. "Is that where you meant to take me?"

"Uh-huh. How come you weren't there?"

Cindy wondered if he'd taken another girl. She glanced up at him quickly. "We decided to go to Gorley's."

"We?"

"Rose and Bill and Mack Gordon and I."

"So Gordon was your date." Peter grinned, but it wasn't his usual grin. It looked as though he had developed a sudden toothache. He took off his glasses and polished them carefully with a clean white handkerchief and put them on again. He nodded. "So that's why you were so anxious for him to have the by-line on that basketball story."

"For goodness' sake," Cindy said hastily, "my dating Mack didn't have anything whatsoever to do with—"

"Forget it." Peter's voice was gruff. He turned back to the table and abruptly his manner became businesslike. "I don't have any rewrites for you at the moment, Cindy, but I do have a rush job for you. I wonder if you'd do the review of the senior class play Friday night? I'd like to have it by next Monday in order to get it in the next issue."

Cindy hesitated, fingering her bracelet uncertainly. She was thinking about Mack, wondering if there was an outside chance that she and Rose might go to the play with Mack and Bill. "What about the Dramatic Club members? Couldn't one of them take care of it?"

"They could, but since it has to be done in a hurry, I'd rather have you. Unless you don't want to be bothered with it."

"No, I'll do it.—Even if it does turn out that I have a date for the play," Cindy thought, "there's no real reason why I can't handle the review, too. It might even make an impression on Mack to see that I have an important assignment like that."

"Okay, then I'll count on you." Peter's eyes crinkled slightly at the corners as he grinned again, more normally. "Being a senior, I have to be in the darned thing. They gave me two lines but I'm not much of an actor, so feel free to pan my performance as much as you like. That's your privilege as drama critic."

"I'll remember that," Cindy said, smiling. Several minutes later she left the library.

During the next few days, however, her mind returned frequently to the conversation with Peter and she couldn't help wondering about his odd reaction to her story. It was true that she had purposely avoided writing anything serious, but hadn't Peter admitted that there was also a place in the *Banner* for humorous pieces? And why had he behaved so peculiarly when she'd told him about dating Mack? Of course Peter had asked her for a date that night himself, which might explain his behavior. On the other hand, he'd seemed cheerful enough when she'd told him in advance that she had another date, so it was hardly consistent for him to be feeling hurt now, was it?

But Peter wasn't the only one who reacted oddly to the news of Cindy's date with Mack. When she told Martha and Jan and Susan, at Weyman's after the Glee Club rehearsal Wednesday afternoon, they didn't seem nearly as impressed as she'd expected them to be.

"So you finally had a date with His Majesty," Susan said, wrinkling her nose and surveying Cindy calmly. "How did you like it?"

"Oh fine." With an effort, Cindy managed to sound as though dates with boys like Mack were an everyday thing in her life.

"Where did you go?" asked Jan.

100

"Gorley's."

"Gorley's?" Martha looked surprised. "What did you think of it?"

Cindy did her best to imitate Rose's disdainful lalugh. "Frankly, I found it rather dull."

"Oh." Martha looked at Jan and Susan and they looked at her. There was a silence—one which lasted so long that Cindy felt compelled to say more. "The crowd was older," she added nervously. Uncertain of what the other girls were thinking, she decided to change to subject. "By the way, I understand that there was some kind of a Teen-Hi affair at the Recreation Center Saturday night. Did you go?"

"All three girls looked a little uncomfortable.

"Yes," Jan said slowly, "we did. I guess we should have mentioned it to you, Cindy, but we figured you probably had a date."

"Besides, we weren't sure you'd be interested," said Susan.

"But we didn't really mean to leave you out," Martha put in quickly. "And that reminds me, Cindy. We're planning to go to the senior class play together. Friday night, and we'd be glad to have you go with us, if you'd care to."

Cindy hesitated. The invitation had caught her by surprise and she didn't know what to do. Although she had talked with Rose several times this week, nothing had been said about the play and it was unlikely that the hoped-for double date would materialize now.

Still, Rose hadn't said anything about *not* going to the play so, as long as there was even a remote chance, wouldn't it be better for Cindy not to commit herself to other plans?

She made up her mind. "I'm sorry, Martha, but I don't believe I'd better plan to go with you. Peter's asked me to do the review—which means that I'll have to go early to do some background work."

"Couldn't we meet you in the auditorium?" asked Jan. "If you're there early, you could save seats for us."

Cindy wondered if she looked as guilty as she felt. "Well, I'll have to sit down front, to take notes and everything, and if there's a big crowd, I doubt that I'd be able to save seats for anyone."

"Oh," said Jan. She and Martha and Susan exchanged another glance.

"But it's true," Cindy told herself later, mentally trying to justify her refusal of the girls' invitation. "I do have to go early and sit down front, and it would probably be hard to save seats for them. On the other hand, if Rose and I go together, I can probably talk her into going early—or, if I can't, at least it won't be so hard to save just one seat. And, even if we don't have dates for the play, we may run into Mack and Bill afterward and, if I'm wtih her, Mack will probably offer to drive us home."

Rationalizing thus, Cindy managed to subdue her feeling of guilt.

She waited all day Thursday for Rose to mention the

play, but Rose didn't say anything. Finally Cindy decided to take matters into her own hands. After her last class, she went to look for Rose and caught her as she was leaving the locker room.

"Hi, Rose," she said nervously. "You aren't meeting Bill or anything, are you?"

"No. He and Mack went off somewhere together, the meanies." Rose looked bored. "Why?"

"Oh, I thought that if you weren't meeting him, we might walk part way home together."

Rose shrugged. "We might as well."

"Just a second till I get my coat." Cindy hurried into the locker room. A few moments later, she rejoined Rose, and the two girls left the building and started home.

They had walked three blocks before Cindy summoned up courage to voice the thought that was uppermost in her mind. "By the way," she said, thrusting her hands into the pockets of her coat so that they wouldn't betray her nervousness, "I've been wondering if you have a date for the play tomorrow night. If you haven't, I thought we might go together."

They were passing the public library where she had worked so hard taking notes to complete Mack's basketball story. Rose's head turned and she gazed at Cindy blankly. "To the play? Do you mean the senior class play?"

"Why, yes," Cindy replied, wondering what other play she *could* mean. "I have to do the review for the

103

Banner, but I haven't made arrangements to go with anyone and I thought that if you didn't have a date, it might be nice for us to go together."

Rose made a face. "I can't think of anything I'd like to do *less*. Personally, I think those school plays are impossible. So dull and amateurish! Once you see one of them, you've seen them all."

"Yes, of course." Cindy smiled to hide her dismay.

"Don't tell me you *want* to go?"

"No, but I have to do the review for the *Banner*."

"Poor you!" Rose laughed and tossed her head. "I'm almost tempted to take pity on you and go along for kicks. I can't, though. Don't tell Bill but I do have a date tomorrow night. It's with a college boy who's coming home for the weekend." She regarded Cindy appraisingly. "Keep quiet about it and next time I may have him bring along a fraternity brother for you."

"I'd like that." Cindy tried to sound enthusiastic but it was hard not to show her disappointment about the play. How stupid of her to assume that a girl as popular as Rose wouldn't have a date for Friday night!

C H A P T E R

10

THE CURTAIN WAS SCHEDULED to rise for Act I of the senior class play at eight o'clock Friday evening. Promptly at seven-fifteen, Cindy gathered up a notebook and several pencils, put on her coat, and started for the school. Having told Martha and Jan and Susan that she had to be there early, she felt that she had to back up her statement, even though she suspected that such an early arrival might make her conspicuous.

When she entered the auditorium twenty minutes later, she found it deserted except for the sophomore students who were acting as ushers and distributing the programs. Nodding to one or two whom she knew by sight, she went quickly down the aisle and took a seat at the end of the second row. Trying hard to look like a busy reporter, she opened her notebook and began to copy the names of the cast from the printed program—a superfluous task, since she would take the program home with her, but at least it gave her something to do. She continued to be acutely conscious of her solitary state, however, and it was a relief when other people began to drift in and when the empty seats beside her were finally taken by a group of giggling freshman girls.

As curtain time drew near, Cindy observed that the atmosphere in the rapidly filling auditorium was very much as it had been on similar occasions in Exeter. The occasional rustling of the curtains as someone peeped out from behind them to look at the audience . . . the beaming faces of the families of members of the cast . . . the identical baskets of flowers at each end of the stage . . . the tuneless soundings of the high school orchestra in the pit . . . she had seen and heard all of these things before, countless times. There was a difference, however. In Exeter, Cindy had always attended such affairs with Sally Baird. Now she was alone. There was no one to whisper to, no one to exchange excited comments with, no one even to look for.

She was alone—and she was lonely.

"But it's my own fault," she reminded herself, trying to shake off her feeling of isolation. "I could be sitting here with Martha and Jan and Susan if I hadn't been so determined to come with Rose. So it isn't as though no one had asked me."

Once, glancing around, she caught sight of Martha and Jan and Susan sitting together near the back of the auditorium, but they didn't seem to see her and there were no empty seats near them.

It seemed a long time before the orchestra struck up the first notes of the *William Tell* Overture. Then, finally, the lights dimmed, the curtains parted, and the play began. Appropriately, since this was Washington's Birthday, the play had a historical background, its action taking place in the colonial period. Cindy had always been interested in American history and presently she was so absorbed in the plot unfolding on the stage that she forgot about being alone.

She particularly liked the costumes. Every detail was authentic, including the buckles on the performers' shoes. And the play had evidently been well rehearsed. Few of the actors forgot their lines, and those who did recovered themselves with only a little prompting.

Peter Holmes, as he had said, had only a minor role but he did very well with it, Cindy thought. He delivered his two lines in a loud, clear voice and he looked almost handsome in his costume, with his brown hair covered by a white wig. Once he shook his head and, with his habitual gesture, reached up to brush back his hair and almost knocked off his wig, but it happened so quickly that Cindy thought few, if any, in the audience noticed. A little later, he looked directly at her and grinned, so she knew he had spotted her in the second row.

Absorbed in the play, she forgot about being alone until the lights came on for the first intermission. Then,

107

as the audience began its appreciative buzz around her, she discovered that she was thirsty. She wondered if she dared get up and go out to the water fountain for a drink.

"I'd better not," she thought. "I must look conspicuous enough already, sitting here alone, with calling *more* attention to myself." So, ignoring her thirst, she pretended to be taking notes all during the intermission. She did the same thing during the second intermission.

When the play was over and the seniors had taken their curtain calls, she quietly closed her notebook and hurried up the aisle, making her way through the crowd of students, parents, and teachers as unobtrusively as she could. She half hoped that she might still run into Martha and Jan and Susan but, by the time she reached the exit, they were nowhere in sight. And, although she saw and spoke to several other girls, none of them asked her to join them.

It wasn't easy to maintain her air of indifference when she felt so very much alone.

Over the weekend, Cindy devoted every spare minute to her review. Trying to capture the over-all atmosphere of the play, she included details about the costumes and scenery as well as a synopsis of the story and comments on the quality of the acting. Remembering what Peter had said about criticizing his performance as much as she liked, she was tempted to say

108

something about his near-accident with his wig, just for fun. But she decided, on second thought, not to mention it for fear of embarrassing him, and instead included his name in a paragraph listing those seniors who had performed well in minor roles.

When she took the review to the school library on Monday, Peter wasn't there, but he came in as she was seating herself at the table. As usual, his arms were loaded with books and papers.

"Hi." He dumped the load on the table, took off his jacket, and sat down beside her. "What did you think of the play?"

Cindy handed him her manuscript. "Read it and see for yourself."

Peter read the review without comment, but when he looked up again his expression was approving. "Nice work, Cindy. I'll rush it right through, so you can look for it in Friday's *Banner*."

"It's not too long?"

"No, about right, I'd say." He grinned. "And thanks for not mentioning the fact that I literally almost blew my top!"

Cindy couldn't resist giggling. "I was tempted to, but I knew you'd blue-pencil it, anyway." Sobering, she went on, "Seriously, I thought you were very good, considering that you had only two lines."

"You'll never know what it cost me to say that much. The way my knees were knocking together, it's a wonder they couldn't be heard all over the auditorium.

I don't have any illusions about my ability as an actor. But thanks for the kind words, anyhow."

"You're welcome." Cindy glanced at the papers on the table. "Anything I can help with?"

"No, I finished the rewrites yesterday." Peter picked up a few of the papers and riffled through them absent-mindedly. "These are unused stories that have been accumulating for several months. Most of them are outdated, but I thought I'd go through them and see if there's anything that can be salvaged for future use."

"Sure I can't help?"

"No, thanks. It's a one-man job. But that reminds me —I've definitely decided to hold your telephone story for the issue after next. Okay?"

"Okay." Feeling somewhat in the way, Cindy pushed back her chair. "I guess I'll run along then. Let me know when you have some more rewrites."

"What's the rush?" Peter asked quickly. "Why not stay and talk for a while?"

"I don't want to keep you from your work."

"This stuff?" Peter shoved the papers aside. "It's not important. Most of it's going to wind up in the wastebasket, anyhow. And there is something I wanted to talk over with you."

"Oh." Cindy settled in her chair, wondering what it was that Peter wanted to talk about. His manner was odd, as though he had something important on his mind. Was he—she frowned as the thought occurred to her—dissatisfied with the way she was handling her *Banner* assignments, in spite of his seeming approval?

Peter seemed to be having trouble getting started. He cleared his throat twice. "I—uh—noticed that you were alone at the play the other night. How come the sudden exclusiveness?"

Surprised, Cindy turned her head so that he couldn't see her expression. Why was he asking? Was he beginning to suspect that she wasn't as popular as she'd been pretending to be? She forced a light, careless laugh. "Exclusiveness? It depends on your point of view. Most of my friends were busy with other things that night and I thought I'd rather go by myself than be bored by dull company."

"Speaking of dull company, how do you find mine? Dull or otherwise?"

"Why do you ask?"

"Well," Peter's ears were fiery red, "I was thinking that if you didn't consider my company too dull, I'd like to take you to the junior prom. Or are you already dated up for it?"

Cindy hesitated. Once again she had been taken by surprise and was torn between two desires. In a way, she longed to accept. It would be wonderful not to have to worry about being invited to the dance, and it wasn't as though she didn't like Peter or wasn't sure about being seen with him. Hadn't Martha and the other girls told her how well he rated? But what if Rose should arrange a double date for the dance with Bill

111

and Mack? Or what if Mack asked Cindy himself? How would she feel if she had to decline Mack's invitation because she'd made a date with Peter?

All of this went through Cindy's mind in a matter of seconds. She took a deep breath and made herself look directly into Peter's eyes. "I'm sorry," she said. "If only you'd ask me a little sooner—" She let it trail off, unfinished.

Peter interpreted her reply as she had hoped he would. "I might have known," he murmured resignedly. He gave her a rueful smile: "Tell me, how far ahead does a guy have to ask to get a date with you?"

"Oh, not so far," Cindy answered, hoping that she looked as confident and sought-after as she was *trying* to look.

"I don't believe it," said Peter. Fortunately, however, he didn't ask who was taking her to the prom.

C H A P T E R

11

HOW WAS THE PLAY?" asked Rose. "Ghastly as usual?"
"Well, it certainly wasn't what you'd call a professional production," Cindy replied evasively. She was ashamed of the evasion but she knew it wouldn't do to admit to Rose that she'd enjoyed the play.

It was Tuesday afternoon and she and Rose were sitting in one of the booths in Weyman's. Cindy had run into Rose after her last class and had suggested coming downtown, in the hope that Rose would say something about the junior prom. Ever since yesterday, she had been wondering if she'd made a mistake in declining Peter's invitation. What if, when the night of the prom rolled around, she should find herself dateless and alone—as she had been on the night of the play?

Rose tossed off her white jacket and smoothed her long, dark hair. "Too bad you weren't with me. We had a simply fabulous time. Heaven only knows what time I got home, but it must have been close to morning."

Cindy sighed involuntarily. From the time they'd entered the drugstore, Rose had been talking about nothing but her Friday night date. At first, Cindy had listened with interest but for the last few minutes it had become increasingly difficult to focus her attention on the rambling discourse. So much of it was repetition! Then, too, the constant references to night clubs and late hours bothered Cindy a little. She kept remembering what Martha and Jan and Susan had said about Rose.

They'd told her that Rose had been expelled from a girls' school last year. Come to think of it, it was odd that Rose had never mentioned it. Cindy was conscious of a sudden stir of curiosity.

She hadn't really intended to ask, but the words seemed to slip out of their own volition. "By the way," she said, as Rose interrupted herself to take a sip of Coke, "I hear that you went to a private school last year. Why didn't you go back? Didn't you like it?"

"I hated it," Rose said flatly. She put down her glass and gazed at Cindy through narrowed eyes. "If you've heard that much, I suppose you've also heard that I was kicked out."

"Well, yes."

"Did anybody tell you why?"

"No, and I didn't ask. I know that most private

114

schools are pretty strict, or at least so I've heard, so I figured that it could have happened for any number of reasons."

"How right you are!" Some of the tension left Rose's voice and she leaned forward, shrugging gracefully. "All I did was stay out once or twice after hours without permission, but the dean made a federal case of it. Not that I cared. I was glad to get away from that prison."

Cindy nodded. "I thought it was probably something like that."

"Of course it caused some local talk," Rose continued. "Some of these Woodmont characters are terribly provincial in their outlook, you'll discover."

"Yes, I suppose they are." Cindy was secretly flattered by Rose's inference that *she* belonged to the more select, broad-minded group of Woodmont residents. Leaning against the back of the booth, she let her mind return to the problem of a date for the prom. What was the best way to let Rose know that she'd like to go with Mack? Perhaps, if she waited long enough, Rose would bring up the subject of her own accord.

Rose, however, seemed to want to talk about everything but the prom. She continued to ramble on about Friday night, and then she launched into a detailed account of a fraternity house party she'd attended a year ago with the same boy.

At length Cindy decided to take matters into her own hands. "Speaking of dances, Rose," she said haltingly, "you're going to the junior prom, aren't you?"

"I haven't decided. Why?"

"Oh, I just thought that if you were, it might be fun for us to go together. Have a double date, I mean. If you go, you'll go with Bill, won't you?"

"If I go," drawled Rose. "Who's your date?"

"I haven't decided yet, either." Cindy flattened her paper straw and twisted it nervously around one finger. "Peter Holmes asked me but I turned him down."

"Smart girl. You'd have a ghastly time with Peter." Rose regarded Cindy speculatively. "If you're not sure of a date, why don't you invite one of your Exeter boy friends? Maybe that one you were telling me about—last year's senior class president."

"Oh, I couldn't!" Cindy gulped, visualizing Bob Evans' reaction if he were to receive an invitation in the mail from "Beanpole" Taylor. He'd probably die laughing!

Rose looked disappointed. "Why not?"

"He's in college now," Cindy replied desperately. "And since the dance is on a Friday night, he wouldn't be able to get here in time."

"Couldn't he cut a few classes?"

"It's too far for him to come, anyway." Cindy's feeling of desperation mounted. She made herself look directly into Rose's eyes. "I was thinking that if you go with Bill, it might be fun for me to go with Mack, since Mack and Bill get along so well together and—and everything."

116

"Oh." Rose's voice was patronizing. "You want me to have Bill get Mack for you, is that it?"

"Well, yes," Cindy admitted, flushing.

"I could ask Bill to mention it to him, I suppose," Rose said without enthusiasm. "It's possible, though, that Mack has asked somebody else by now."

"I know. But just in case he hasn't, would—would you mind saying something to Bill?"

"All right." Rose's smile was superior. "I'll see what I can do."

"Thanks a million." Cindy was relieved, but she was also embarrassed. She wished that Rose hadn't made it necessary for her to *ask*.

But at least she had instigated some action. Now all that she could do was wait and hope.

Waiting wasn't easy. During the following days, Cindy continued to hover around Rose, talking with her on the slightest pretext whenever the opportunity presented itself. But Rose didn't say another word about the prom, and somehow Cindy couldn't summon up the courage to mention it herself. Rose's silence worried her, however, because everyone else was talking almost constantly about the dance. Everywhere that Cindy went it seemed that girls were gathering together in groups of two and three and four to talk about their gowns and dates. Before Glee Club rehearsal on Wednesday Martha and Jan and Susan stopped her in the aisle to announce that they were going with junior classmates.

"That's swell!" Cindy exclaimed, wondering what they would think if they knew that she didn't have a date for the dance. Whatever happened, she mustn't let them know.

The inevitable question came a moment later. "Incidentally, Cindy," asked Susan, "who's your date?"

Cindy swallowed. "You'll see."

"Somebody from Exeter?" guessed Jan.

"I'll bet it is." Martha looked wise. "Probably that fellow who was last year's senior class president."

"Cindy, are you bringing a *college man?*" Susan cried breathlessly.

Cindy stood very straight and did her best to look mysterious. "You'll see," she repeated, and hastily changed the subject. "But you haven't told me yet what you're planning to wear."

Martha and Jan both said that they had bought new dresses. Martha's was white faille and Jan's was pink chiffon.

"Not me," sighed Susan. "I'll have to wear my green tulle again. It was new last fall and I can't buy another one until next year." Her freckled face brightened. "Anyway, since it's green it will tie in with our St. Patrick's Day decorations. Which reminds me, Cindy— thanks for the suggestion about the balloons. I passed it along to the rest of the decorations committee and they liked it and are going to use it. Hope you don't mind our repeating something you've done before."

"Not at all," Cindy murmured.

"We're going to use St. Patrick's Day hats as center-pieces for the punch table," Susan continued blithely. "We'll cut holes in the tops and fill them with forsythia —if we can find some forsythia branches and force them to bloom by then. If not, we'll have to use ivy, I guess, or—"

"Stop chattering, Sue," Martha interrupted, laughing. "Give Cindy a chance to tell us what she's going to wear. What about it, Cindy? Going to knock our eyes out with something spectacular?"

"I—I haven't decided yet," Cindy stammered.

Luckily, the rehearsal began before anyone could ask her again about her date.

As the week went along, the junior prom continued to be the number one topic of conversation in Wood-mont High, and Cindy's inner anxiety continued to mount correspondingly. Now, in addition to hovering around Rose, she began to watch Mack closely, hoping for some word or sign that would indicate his inten-tions regarding the dance. But Mack's manner toward her was as it had always been—polite but remote. And Rose continued to behave as though she'd forgotten that there even was to be such an affair as a junior prom. The only thing on Rose's mind, it seemed, was a trip she was planning to take this weekend. She was leaving immediately after school on Friday to visit the girl who had been her roommate at boarding school.

"It's not far from where you used to live," she re-

119

marked to Cindy in passing. "I'll ask my friend if she knows anyone in Exeter. You and she may have some mutual friends."

Cindy's mind was so preoccupied with the prom that the remark didn't fully register. "Maybe we do," she murmured absently.

By Friday, her anxiety had reached a peak. Late that morning, the new issue of the *Banner* was distributed and it contained her review of the senior class play. But neither the sight of her by-line in the paper nor the compliments of those who noticed the review did much to boost Cindy's sagging morale. What good would her temporary prominence do her if, a week from tonight, she didn't have a date for the prom?

At noon, picking listlessly at her lunch, she decided that it was time to face facts. There could be only one explanation for Rose's continued silence. It must be that Rose—or Bill, at Rose's suggestion—had asked Mack about the double date and Mack had refused. And Rose hadn't told Cindy because she didn't want to hurt her feelings.

It was a bitter pill to swallow, but it was the only explanation that made sense. Convinced that she had found the right answer, Cindy told herself that she didn't care. If Mack didn't like her well enough to take her to the dance, it was all right with her. For a moment she was tempted to go to Peter and tell him that she had changed her mind but, upon reflection, she gave up the idea. In all probability Peter had asked another girl now, so why embarrass him?

"I guess I'll just have to be sick next Friday," she thought, regarding herself forlornly in the bathroom mirror as she brushed her teeth after lunch. "Which won't be very hard to do. The way I feel right now, I probably *will* be sick."

And then, when Cindy had almost given up hope, the unexpected happened. She had returned to school and was walking down the corridor toward her home room when Mack came strolling up to her.

"Hi, there," he said with his careless grin. "Clever review you had in the *Banner* this morning."

"Thank you." Cindy nodded coldly and started on, but Mack blocked her way.

"Hey, wait a minute. I want to talk to you."

Cindy's breath seemed to catch in her throat. "What about?"

"What's this I hear about us going to the junior prom together?" Mack demanded.

Unable to look at him, Cindy lowered her eyes. It was all that she could do to keep her voice steady. "It seems to me that I did hear something along those lines."

"Well, what do you think?" Mack's tone was non-committal.

Cindy hesitated. Surely he wasn't going to make her ask him, was he? She glanced up quickly but Mack's face was as expressionless as his voice. "What do *you* think?" she countered.

Mack shrugged. "We might as well, if Rose and Bill are going. As Rose says, it ought to be good for a few laughs. What do you say? Shall we make it a date?"

To her own surprise, Cindy managed to sound as disinterested as he did. "It's all right with me."

"Okay." Mack was silent for a second or two, apparently going over something in his mind. "The dance is scheduled to start at nine. If I don't see you again before then, I'll be up for you next Friday around that time. Okay?"

"Okay," Cindy agreed. With another careless smile, Mack turned away, heading for the gym. She made herself walk slowly until he had entered the gym and was out of sight. But then she couldn't resist doing a quick hop, skip, and jump. It had happened! Patience and persistence had paid off and she was going to the junior prom with Mack Gordon!

CHAPTER

12

CINDY HAD NEVER GONE to a formal dance in Exeter and she didn't own an evening gown, so, after a Saturday morning consultation with her mother, she went downtown to look for one. She spent the better part of the morning going from one shop to another and finally found two dresses she liked. One of them—a black crepe which had been reduced in price because it was a winter model—was Cindy's real preference because it made her look a little older. But it was almost backless, which she knew her mother would never approve, so at length she chose the other—a powder-blue taffeta. It had a snug bodice and full skirt, with a cerise-colored petticoat, and a long velvet sash in the same shade of cerise.

In the shoe department of the same shop, she found white Shantung slippers which could be tinted any shade and were available with either flat or high heels. Exulting in the knowledge that she could forgo her customary flats, since Mack was so tall, she promptly bought a pair "with heels" and arranged to have them dyed cerise to match her sash and petticoat.

That night she tried the gown on for her parents, twirling and pirouetting in front of them so that they could see how full the skirt was and how the sash floated out when she whirled. Both her mother and father approved of her choice.

"It's lovely, Lucinda." Her mother lifted the hem to see how well the seams were made. "I don't believe we'll have to make a single alteration."

"Young Gordon's a lucky boy," her father said, beaming. "I only wish I were young enough to take you to the dance myself!"

When she took the gown off, Cindy hung it inside out on the hanger and covered it carefully with a plastic garment bag.

At school the following Monday, Rose confirmed their double date. "Sorry I didn't get around to telling you before this," she said casually, "but I forgot about the prom until almost the end of the week and then I had to wait until Bill had checked with Mack. And, as you know, I was away over the weekend."

Cindy explained that she had already talked with Mack.

"Incidentally," Rose went on, "my friend—the one I

visited—has been in Exeter, and she tells me that it's not a very large town."

"No, but it's nice," Cindy said quickly.

"I dare say your opinion of any town depends upon the people you know there." Rose gave Cindy an odd, knowing glance. "You and your friends probably managed to dig up plenty of excitement."

Nothing could be further from the truth, but Cindy refrained from saying so. Anxious to get away from dangerous ground, she said, "Mack's going to pick me up around nine o'clock Friday night, so we'll probably be stopping by for you and Bill a few minutes later."

Rose shook her head. "No, Bill's taking his father's car. Not that it matters. We can follow you or you can follow us."

Cindy did some quick thinking. It seemed a shame to go to the dance alone when Mack's station wagon could carry so many passengers. "Why don't we take some of the others? Martha and Jan and Susan are all going to the dance, and if we split them and their dates between the two cars, we'd have room for all of them."

"Are you kidding?" Rose's eyes were suddenly cold, her voice disdainful. "Mack and Bill would be furious if we asked them to take that crowd along. What if the dance is a flop and we decide not to stay?"

"Oh." Cindy realized that once again she'd said the wrong thing. "Of course," she murmured apologetically. "Now that I think about it, I can see that it would be a mistake." The apology came hard, however, and she felt disloyal for not coming to the defense of Martha and Jan and Susan.

But it was Rose who had arranged the date with Mack for the prom—Rose who had it in her power to arrange future dates with Mack. So if Cindy had to make a choice between Rose and the other girls, what could she do but align herself with Rose?

With mingled gratitude and hope, Cindy began to devote herself to the task of cementing her friendship with Rose, seeking her out between classes, walking home with her after school, and doing everything she could to indicate that she wanted to be "best friends." Rose, in turn, seemed to find Cindy's company agreeable. At least she made no attempt to discourage it, although there were times when Cindy wondered whether Rose was simply putting up with her because she was a good listener.

There were times, too, when Cindy worried about Martha and Jan and Susan. As she began to identify herself more and more closely with Rose, there was a perceptible change in her relationship with the other girls. They weren't exactly hostile, but their manner became constrained. She particularly noticed it Wednesday afternoon when she went downtown with them after the Glee Club rehearsal. None of the three girls had much to say to her even when, in an effort to smooth relationships, she discarded her air of mystery and told them she was going to the dance with Mack.

"Double dating with Rose and Bill?" Susan wanted to know.

"Why, yes," Cindy answered.

"That's what I thought," said Susan and, again, she and Martha and Jan lapsed into one of their peculiar silences.

Cindy told herself that their reaction wasn't unexpected, that she'd known all along how they felt about Rose. But she wished she didn't have an occasional twinge of misgiving. She liked Martha and Jan and Susan; in her heart she liked them better than Rose. Certainly she was far more at ease with them than with Rose.

With Rose she was always on guard, always trying to match her bored sophistication. Sometimes, walking with Rose down one of the school corridors, or sitting in a booth at Weyman's listening to her endless chatter, Cindy would find herself thinking, "Is this what I really want? Now that I seem to be succeeding in my new role, am I happy?

"Of course it's what I want," she would reassure herself promptly. "And of course I'm happy. If I hadn't pretended to be popular and poised, Rose would never have bothered with me, and if I hadn't become friendly with Rose, I'd never, never be going to the prom with Mack.

"And what girl *wouldn't* be happy to be going to a big dance with Mack Gordon?"

The days merged into one another and finally it was

Friday, the day of the prom. Mack hadn't said anything to Cindy all week, but he stopped her in the corridor that morning to say that he'd call for her at nine and, after that, she was so excited that she couldn't think of anything but the dance. Fortunately the teachers all seemed to be in an understanding mood and didn't demand too much of anyone in classes.

That evening, as soon as dinner was over, she went upstairs and began to dress. She had washed her hair the night before but, dissatisfied with the way it looked, she re-dampened it and combed it diligently in front of the bathroom mirror. She gave herself a manicure, took a leisurely bath, using the bubble bath that she saved for special occasions, and finally, just before nine, climbed carefully into the powder-blue dress.

Mack didn't arrive until nine-thirty, but when Cindy saw how handsome he looked in his dinner jacket, she promptly forgave him for being late. The excited pounding of her heart seemed to double in tempo and it was all that she could do to murmur "Thank you" when Mack complimented her on her appearance. Nor could she manage more than a few words during the drive to Rose's house.

They arrived there just as Rose and Bill were leaving. Bill's father's car was a large sedan and, observing its size, Cindy couldn't help thinking again about Martha and Jan and Susan and their dates. Were they also riding to the dance or were they walking? Huriedly she dismissed the pinprick of worry from her mind. Nothing must spoil tonight!

It still seemed almost unbelievable—"Beanpole" Taylor, the shy nonentity of Exeter, going to a dance with the best-looking boy in Woodmont High! What if she'd had to scheme a little to accomplish it? The result was worth the effort, wasn't it? Mack was so prominent and such a good dancer that she was sure to have a wonderful time. But she'd have to be very, very careful not to do anything to betray the fact that this was her first dance. Probably the wisest course would be to follow Rose's lead all evening.

By the time they arrived at the high school gym, Cindy was almost in a daze. Following Rose into the locker room to hang up her coat, she felt as though she were walking in a dream. She experienced a momentary setback when she saw Rose's gown; it was flame red and had even less of a back than the black crepe she'd admired downtown. For a second, Cindy felt awkward and schoolgirlish in her powder-blue taffeta, and she wondered if Mack would notice the vast difference between Rose's dress and her own. But then she and Rose rejoined the two boys and went on into the gym and, in a new surge of anticipation, Cindy forgot about clothes.

The decorations were beautiful! Everywhere she looked there were giant green shamrocks, green-and-white crepe-paper streamers and, overhead, clouds of green balloons. Sometime during the evening, the balloons would be released and come drifting down among the dancers. Which one of them held Cindy's name? Shivering, she looked across the gym and spied the long, green-covered table, its center adorned with St. Patrick's Day hats from the tops of which a profusion of yellow blossoms was sprouting. She was glad, for Susan's sake, to see that the forsythia had bloomed.

Several teachers were sitting together in the corner of the gym nearest the punch table. Glancing at them, Cindy noticed that the group included two of her favorite teachers, Miss Ferguson and Miss Clarke. She mustn't forget to speak to them and thank them for chaperoning the dance. Her mother had particularly warned her about that. But she'd better wait and speak to them when Rose did.

The two couples had arrived in the middle of a dance. They stood in the doorway for a few minutes, looking around, then Mack said abruptly, "Well, shall we dance?" And, without waiting for a reply, he led Cindy onto the floor.

Cindy was thankful that she had danced with him before; otherwise, dazed as she was, she would never have been able to follow him. As it was, she had to concentrate hard to keep from stumbling, and didn't have much chance to look at the other dancers, although she did see Susan dance by in the arms of a junior classmate.

"I'm at the junior prom with Mack Gordon . . . I'm at the junior prom with Mack Gordon!" The words ran through Cindy's mind like the refrain of a song. It didn't seem quite real; she still felt as though she were dreaming.

She danced that number and the next with Mack. They exchanged a dance with Rose and Bill, and then she danced with Mack again. It wasn't until near the end of her third dance with Mack that Cindy began to sense that there was something wrong—that something about the prom wasn't proceeding according to her expectations. Even then she couldn't figure out what it was.

She had her first inkling of understanding when she and Mack rejoined Rose and Bill. As at the end of the preceding dances, the two couples formed a small group at the edge of the dance floor and were standing there, talking, when Cindy happened to glance over Mack's shoulder and noticed that they were some distance from their classmates.

"We're not mingling with the other kids," she thought, startled. "Rose and Mack and Bill probably don't realize it, but they're acting as though everyone else here is a stranger. I wonder if I ought to say something about it. We should speak to the others, at least. If we don't, they may think we're snubbing them."

She saw Martha and her escort in the center of a gay group which had congregated near the bandstand. Catching her eye, Cindy nodded and smiled and Martha nodded in return. But neither she nor any of her friends made any move toward Cindy's group, and when Cindy turned back to her companions, she understood why. All three faces—Rose's and Mack's and Bill's—were wearing almost the same supercilious expression. Clearly, they didn't care to be joined by anyone!

"What a band," Rose complained loudly. "I wonder what fourth-rate night club they escaped from?"

"What did you expect?" drawled Mack. "You know they never get a decent orchestra for these high school brawls."

"No, but I was hoping for some improvements by now," Rose retorted.

"Same old music, same old routine!" Bill made a resigned gesture.

Cindy wished that they would lower their voices. All three of her companions were talking so loudly that she was sure they could be heard halfway across the gym. In an effort to change the subject, she said hesitantly, "At least it's a large turnout."

Rose's eyes swept disdainfully around the room. "*Too* large. How some of these characters can imagine they're having a good time at a juvenile affair like this, I'll never know."

Mack laughed. "Maybe that's because most of them *are* juvenile." He glanced at Cindy. "How about it, Cindy? Ever get embroiled in anything like this back in your old home town?"

Luckily the music began again just then and Cindy was spared the necessity of making a reply. But from that moment, most of the magic was gone for her. And her happiness dwindled steadily as the evening wore on. Taking her cue from Rose and Bill and Mack, she tried hard to behave as they did, alternately pretending boredom and indifference. But underneath she was confused and embarrassed. Didn't her companions realize how conspicuous they were making themselves —and her—with their superior airs? And what had happened to her dream—the one in which Cindy Taylor, at the junior prom, had been the center of an admiring throng, the cynosure of all eyes?

She was the cynosure of a great many eyes, all right, but not in the way she had dreamed. Thank goodness, Peter Holmes wasn't at the dance. She could just imagine how *he'd* have looked at her.

Her embarrassment grew. When the punch was served, Rose and the two boys refused to join the long line at the table and decided to go outside for a cigarette, instead. Cindy felt that she had no choice but to go with them, though she didn't smoke, but when they returned to the gym, she felt more conspicuous than ever. She was sure that everyone had noticed their absence and was speculating about where they had been.

Once, between dances, she suggested going over and speaking to the chaperones, but Rose said. "Whatever for?" and Mack and Bill stared at her as though she'd lost her mind. And Cindy couldn't summon up the courage to leave them and walk across the floor by herself.

It was a relief when, shortly after eleven, Mack said, "Has everybody had enough? I think it's time to ditch this brawl."

"I'm ready," Rose agreed. "What about you, Cindy?"

Cindy nodded silently and, a moment later, followed Rose toward the locker room. She didn't turn until she'd reached the doorway of the gym, where she paused and glanced up, just once, at the clouds of green balloons, still poised high above the heads of the dancers. Which one of them held Cindy Taylor's name?

With a wistful sigh, she turned again and went to get her coat.

CHAPTER

13

It was raining when they came out—not a hard rain but a cold, steady March drizzle, which had coated the pavement with a wet, greasy-looking film. Shivering, Cindy buttoned her coat collar around her neck and wished that she had something to put over her head. It would be the last straw if she caught cold tonight.

Bill's sedan and Mack's station wagon were parked side by side near the end of the block. "Where to?" Rose asked, as the foursome paused between the two cars. "Anybody have any bright ideas?"

"How about the Eagles' Nest?" Bill suggested.

"What's the Eagles' Nest?" asked Cindy.

Mack laughed. "A night club on Route 22." He turned to Bill. "Sounds okay to me."

"Me, too." Rose's voice was more enthusiastic than it had been all evening. "Cindy?"

Disappointed by the dance, Cindy longed to go home. Yet she was still reluctant to say or do anything that might antagonize Mack. "How far is it?" she asked uncertainly.

"Only ten miles or so," Mack replied. "We can be there in less than ten minutes."

"In this crate of yours?" scoffed Bill. "Who do you think you're kidding?"

Mack bristled. "Any old time it can't beat that pile of junk you're driving!" Suddenly he snapped his fingers. "I'll give you two to one that we make it to the Eagles' Nest before you do!"

"You're on!" Bill grabbed Rose's arm and yanked open a door of the sedan. "Come on, Rose. We're going to race Mack to the club!"

Cindy found herself being propelled into the station wagon. There was a sudden roar of motors and, seconds behind Bill, Mack pulled away from the curb, made a wide U-turn in the middle of the street, and skidded around the corner, heading for Market Street and Route 22.

For the first few seconds Cindy was too startled to think, but as the station wagon hurtled along the dark streets, she became conscious of a mounting fear. She had read countless newspaper stories about tragic accidents resulting from hot-rod racing by reckless teenagers. Only two years ago, an Exeter boy had been

136

killed and another boy seriously injured in a "drag" race which had taken place on the highway not far from town.

She thought of what her father had said at the time: "It's a vicious practice, Cindy, and don't you ever forget it. Some of these irresponsible teen-age drivers forget that *lives* are involved."

The accident had made a deep impression on Cindy and she had vowed then and there never to forget her father's warning. Yet, here she was taking part in a race which would be dangerous even on a clear night. On a night like tonight, with vision obscurred by the drizzling rain and with the roads as wet and slippery as they were, it was insane!

"But I don't dare let on that I'm frightened," she thought, clinging precariously to the edge of the seat and staring at the red taillight of Bill's sedan ahead. "If I do, Mack will think I'm a coward, especially compared with Rose, and he'll probably laugh at me. Or worse, he might be disgusted and not want to have anything more to do with me. Anyway, we aren't really going so fast—it only seems that way because we're still in town. And ten miles isn't so far; surely nothing can happen in such a short distance."

Determinedly she relaxed her hold on the edge of the seat and tore her gaze away from the windshield. She wouldn't even consider the possibility of an accident; she'd think about the prom instead.

But there was not much comfort for Cindy in her

memories of the prom. She kept thinking about Martha and Jan and Susan . . . Miss Ferguson . . . the green balloons which had been so near and now seemed so far away. Why had Rose and Mack and Bill been so rude? Why had they sneered at the other students? Didn't they care whether they hurt peoples' feelings or not?

"I guess they don't," Cindy thought worriedly. "I guess if you're *really* sophisticated, the way they are, you don't even think about other people. But I do. Maybe I shouldn't but I do."

The two cars had reached the highway now and, as Mack's foot came down hard on the throttle, Cindy glanced at the speedometer and stiffened again, involunarily. They were going sixty-five . . . seventy . . . seventy-five, and the distance between the station wagon and Bill's sedan was starting to lessen. And still the speedometer needle climbed higher. It was hovering close to eighty now. Every now and then the station wagon would give a sickening lurch as one of its tires skidded momentarily on the slick highway. The windshield was fogged and it was impossible to see much except the faint red glimmering of the sedan's taillight and an occasional blinding flash as a car from the opposite direction roared past.

"Please, I wish you wouldn't go so fast!" The words seemed to tumble from Cindy's lips of their own accord.

"What's the matter? Scared?" In the dim light from

the dashboard, Mack's face was flushed and excited.

"A little." Cindy's eyes went to the speedometer again and she shuddered. "Won't you please, *please* slow down?"

"What, and have Bill think he beat me in that old clunker he's driving? Not on your life!" Mack laughed and the speedometer needle edged higher. "Relax. We've almost caught him. I think I can take him before we get to that next bend in the road."

Far from reassuring Cindy, the words sent a fresh shiver of terror down her spine. She braced her feet against the floorboards and squeezed her eyes tightly shut. "Nothing's going to happen," she told herself frantically. "Nothing's going to happen—"

But she couldn't shut out the throbbing roar of the engine or the humming sound of the tires on the wet, slick road.

She opened her eyes again and almost cried out. They were gaining rapidly on the sedan now. The red taillight was growing brighter every second . . . it was coming closer and closer . . . they were almost up to it. Mack was swerving the station wagon to pass Bill and the two cars were abreast, going into the bend.

What happened next happened so quickly that there wasn't time to think. One instant, Cindy saw the branch of a tree lying directly ahead of them in the road—the next instant, the station wagon gave another sickening lurch and suddenly spun out of control, veering away from the road and heading for a concrete culvert which lay directly in its path.

There was a loud grinding and squealing noise as Mack tried to apply the brakes, a series of jolting bumps as the rear wheels left the road, and then, with a suddenness which threw Cindy forward and slammed her head against the windshield, the station wagon came to a stop, inches short of the culvert.

For a minute there was no sound in the station wagon except the faint splash of rain on the roof. Then Cindy reached up gingerly to feel her head and, simultaneously, Mack relaxed his grip on the steering wheel.

"Are you okay?" he asked.

Cindy's head was beginning to ache but to her relief, the skin wasn't broken. "I'm all right. Are you?"

"Yes, sure." Mack was silent for another second or two. "Well, let's see if the wagon still runs." He put the car into reverse and slowly began to back away from the culvert. "Everything seems to be okay. Some fun!"

The station wagon shot forward again.

A hundred yards ahead, Bill had stopped the sedan in front of a deserted service station. As Mack pulled in behind him, the sedan doors opened and Bill and Rose came running back.

Mack rolled down his window. "Nothing to get excited about. We're okay. But you'd better hop in while we decide what to do. No use standing out there getting wet."

Rose and Bill climbed into the station wagon. Bill was shaking his head. "Man, are you lucky! I thought you were going to plow into that culvert for sure!"

"Who, me?" Mack shrugged and lit a cigarette. "I've had lots of closer shaves. Anyhow, you'll have to admit that this old buggy of mine has what it takes. If it hadn't been for that darned branch in the road, I'd be a mile ahead of you by now."

"That's what you think! Just because I had sense enough to slow down for that curve and you didn't—"

"Stop it, you two!" To Cindy's astonishment, Rose was laughing. "I'm willing to call the race a draw. The point is, what do we do now?"

"Why not go on to the Eagles' Nest?" Mack said calmly.

"Why not?" Rose's voice was similarly nonchalant.

"Suits me," said Bill.

Cindy could hardly believe her ears. How could they talk about going on to the night club just as though nothing had happened? It was the last thing in the world that *she* wanted to do. Her head was throbbing and she was still half numb with fright. One terrifying thought kept occurring to her over and over again: *What if they had met another car, coming from the opposite direction, back there in the bend?*

She took a deep, quivering breath. "Not me. I want to go home."

"What's wrong?" Bill spoke first. "You're not hurt, are you?"

"No, but I bumped my head against the windshield and I'm getting a headache. Anyway, I feel sort of shaky."

"For Heaven's sake, Cindy!" Rose said scornfully. "Don't tell me you're chickening out on us!"

It was the type of remark which ordinarily would have worried Cindy, implying as it did that she wasn't measuring up to the standard set by the others. But now she was too upset to care. And all at once she was tired of pretending. "Call it that if you want to," she said quietly, "but I don't want to go anywhere but home. If you won't take me there, I—I guess I'll just have to get out and walk."

"You can skip the dramatics." Mack sounded half surprised, half annoyed. "If that's the way you feel, I'll take you home." He turned to Rose and Bill. "Why don't you go on to the club? I'll run her home and come back and meet you there."

"Okay." Bill reached for the door handle. "Come on, Rose."

"I'm coming." Rose started to get out and paused. "But I won't forget this, Cindy. Don't think for a minute that you're fooling *me!*" She flounced out of the station wagon. A moment later, the sedan roared off down the road.

As soon as it had disappeared, Mack turned the station wagon around and headed back toward Woodmont. He didn't say a word all the way into town but he drove with exaggerated slowness, and Cindy knew that it was his way of showing her what he thought of her. When they arrived at her house, he was polite enough about walking up to the door with her, but the instant she had the door open, he said good night and hurried off, obviously eager to rejoin Rose and Bill.

Cindy was relieved to find that her mother and father had gone to bed. It was only a little after twelve and she had been afraid that they might still be up. And, shaken as she was, she didn't feel up to facing them and answering the questions they would inevitably ask about the dance.

She turned out the light that had been left burning for her, and tiptoed quietly up to her bedroom. Taking off the powder-blue dress, she surveyed it carefully and was thankful to see that it had suffered no damage in the near accident. Sighing as she remembered the anticipation with which she'd put it on, she hung it in the closet, finished undressing, and climbed into her pajamas.

She took an aspirin tablet before she went to bed and presently the throbbing ache in her head began to diminish. But she couldn't fall asleep. She kept reliving the frightening ride through the rainy night; each time she closed her eyes, she could hear the station wagon's screaming brakes and see the concrete culvert looming up ahead of the car, terrifyingly close. At length, in an effort to lull herself to sleep, she deliberately forced the memory of the race from her mind and tried to think, instead, about the prom. But, as before, her memories of the dance brought little solace. What a far cry it had been from the enchanted evening of her dreams!

If only Rose and Mack and Bill hadn't taken such a superior attitude! If only they'd mingled with the other students and pretended, at least, to be having a good time! But they hadn't. They hadn't even noticed how much their behavior was embarrassing Cindy.

"But I *was* embarrassed," Cindy thought. "I hated snubbing the teachers and the other kids, and I hated the way everybody kept looking at us. The trouble is, I'm not the least bit like Rose. Maybe I've managed to convince everyone that I'm as sophisticated as she is, but I'm not. I'm only pretending. And a lot of good it's done me. If anything, I'm not as well off as I was in Exeter. At least I had Sally Baird's friendship there."

"Not as well off as I was in Exeter." Suddenly Cindy sat up and turned on her bed light. Blinking, she propped a pillow behind her head and repeated the thought aloud in a small, half-amazed whisper. *"Not as well off as I was in Exeter!"* The longer she thought about it, the more she realized it was true. Maybe her pose had succeeded, but her plan had not. Far from becoming popular in Woodmont, she hadn't made *any* close friends. She hadn't even succeeded in interesting Mack. He had dated her and he had taken her to the prom, but he had done so only as a favor to Rose.

"When it comes right down to it," Cindy mused, "the only thing I've accomplished is a sort of psuedo friend-

144

ship with Rose. And, judging from the way she flounced out of the station wagon, even that's ended after tonight."

Frowning, she thought of the magazine article she had read in Exeter that had inspired her attempted transformation. Somehow or other, she must have misinterpreted its advice. But how? Surely it had been no mistake to try to improve her appearance, had it? But then why had she failed? Why hadn't things turned out as well for her as they had for the beautiful Margaret?

She had gone too far. The instant the thought came to Cindy, she knew she had hit upon the right, the only possible answer. In trying to follow the magazine article's advice, she had gone overboard, had gone to extremes which the author of the article had never intended. She had tried to assume a new personality completely foreign to her nature and, as a result, had succeeded only in confusing everyone. How could her new classmates be expected to understand and like her if she neither understood nor particularly liked herself?

But if that were true, why keep on pretending? Wouldn't it be better to discard the pretense before any further damage was done? Perhaps the real Cindy Taylor would never be a belle, but she could at least be relaxed and at ease. She wouldn't have to be forever on guard, forever trying. She might even, in time, win a few *genuine* friends, girls like Martha and Jan and Susan.

"I guess it's the only thing to do," Cindy thought,

reaching up and snapping off the light. "Might as well face it—I don't have much choice, anyway. So what if it does mean giving up a few dreams? They weren't the sort of dreams which could ever possibly have come true. . . ."

A few minutes later, she was sound asleep.

C H A P T E R

14

"How was the prom?" Cindy's mother asked.

"Oh fine," Cindy replied automatically. She was in the kitchen eating a late breakfast and her mother had just come up from the basement with a load of freshly laundered towels in her arms.

Mrs. Taylor put the towels away and poured herself a cup of coffee. She sat down on the other side of the table. "Did everyone like your new dress?"

"I think so." Cindy tried to think of something else she could tell her mother about the dance. "The decorations were lovely—all in green for St. Patrick's Day, since it comes this month. Susan Greer was on the decorating committee and they did a wonderful job."

"I'm sure they did." Her mother smiled interestedly. "I was awake when you came in, but didn't call to you

147

because I didn't want to disturb your father. I'm glad Mack didn't keep you out too late."

"Yes." Cindy took a bite of toast and wondered whether she ought to tell her mother about the race and near accident. She decided not to. Nobody had been hurt and there was no point in worrying Mother and Dad about Mack's driving when she'd probably never go out with him again.

In the cold light of day, her decision of last night was unchanged; if anything, she was more determined than ever to discard her pretense of sophistication. But as she buttered another piece of toast, it occurred to her that Mack's inevitable disappearance from her life might arouse some family curiosity. "Speaking of Mack," she said casually, "I hope you and Dad aren't getting any funny notions about him. The fact that he happened to take me to the dance doesn't mean a thing, you know. Mack dates a lot of different girls."

Her mother carefully stirred cream into her coffee. "To tell the truth, Cindy, I think it's just as well. Mack has nice manners and he comes from a good family but he seems rather old for you."

"He's the same age I am!"

"Yes, I know, but he gives the impression of being older. Also, he seems somewhat superficial to me, although perhaps I think that because I don't know him well."

Her mother didn't like Mack! It was obvious not only from her tone of voice but from her expression. Cindy had trouble concealing her amazement. "Well," she said slowly, "it doesn't really matter. It will probably be a long time before he asks me for another date—if ever."

She spoke with a serenity she was far from feeling, however. It was the one thing about her decision which bothered her—the strong probability that, with the dropping of her pose, she was eliminating her last hope of interesting Mack. In spite of everything—his behavior at the dance, his reckless driving, and his rudeness when he'd brought her home—she was still attracted to him and she knew it in her heart.

"But I'll simply have to get over it," she thought, as she stood up and carried her plate to the sink. "Mack's never shown any interest in me; he'd never have dated me if it hadn't been for Rose. So I'll simply have to get over it."

She repeated the admonition to herself many times that day, but she couldn't seem to banish Mack from her thoughts.

Sunday was one of those rare March days with a temperature in the fifties and a sun as bright and yellow as a giant dandelion. Late in the afternoon, Cindy went outside and played with the two young Thomas children next door, showing them how to use an archery set they'd been given for Christmas. On the way back to the house, she paused beside the lilac bushes and noticed that there were small brown buds on the tip of every branch. "As though they can hardly wait to burst into bloom," she thought, breaking off a twig and inspecting it idly; and the thought gave a new lift to her spirits. Surely, with spring just around the corner, nothing in the world could be too far out of kilter. She'd made a bad start in Woodmont with her misguided attempt to change her personality, but now that she was aware of her mistake, she could correct it without too much trouble.

When Cindy woke up Monday morning, however, she found that the hint of springtime had vanished overnight. With typical March treachery, the weather had turned cold and rainy and, simultaneously, her spirits plummeted downward. She felt as cheerless and lonely as the forlorn sparrow that was hopping around the front lawn when she went out to get the morning's milk.

She decided to wear her new raincoat to school because it had a jaunty military cut which had made her feel brave and dashing when she'd tried it on in the store. But today even the new raincoat didn't do much to improve her spirits. All she could think of as she splashed along the rain-washed sidewalks was the immediate future. What sort of a reception was awaiting her at school?

Rose would probably still be peeved at her because of her refusal to go on to the Eagles' Nest Friday night. And Mack and Bill would probably be more indifferent than ever. But what about the others? Would they be resentful because she'd slighted them at the dance? The

150

closer Cindy drew to the high school building, the more worried she became.

She knew as soon as she walked into her home room that her fears had been warranted. Rose glanced at her, frowned, and looked quickly away. Neither Mack nor Bill bothered to look up. What really startled her, however, was the behavior of Martha and Jan and Susan. As Cindy went to her desk, all three girls glanced at her but not one of them smiled or spoke.

It was an even colder reception than Cindy had anticipated. "But no colder than I deserve," she thought, taking out the books for her first class. "Even before the dance, I wasn't very nice to Martha and Jan and Susan. I refused to go to the senior class play with them and I've made it pretty obvious recently that I preferred Rose's company to theirs. They have no way of knowing that I didn't really mean it, or that I've decided to stop pretending now. It's up to me to show them how I feel."

As the bell rang, she fixed a friendly smile on her face and squared her shoulders determinedly. Sometime during the morning she would make a particular point of speaking to the three girls, perhaps on the pretext of asking about a lesson assignment. And when she did, she would do everything she could to indictae that she was sorry about the way she had treated them and wanted very much to start all over again.

She kept the smile on her face all morning and she did her best, whenever she had a chance, to attract the attention of Martha, Jan, or Susan. Long before noon, however, Cindy began to realize that all three girls were avoiding her, and the knowledge hurt even though she felt that she deserved the snub.

"I'll have to be patient," she told herself. "After all, I can't expect them to come running the instant I change my mind."

Then, as Cindy was on her way to the locker room at noon, she met Rose and, on the spur of the moment, decided to attempt a reconciliation with her. "Even if Rose and I don't have much in common," she thought, "there's no reason for us to be enemies."

"Hi, Rose," she said. "Glad I ran into you. I've been hoping I'd have a chance to talk with you privately."

Rose halted and regarded her coldly. "What about?"

"About us. I can't help wondering what I've done to make you so mad at me."

"You know very well what you've done." Rose's voice was as cold as her eyes. "What's the big idea of running out on me Friday night?"

"I didn't run out on you. I was frightened, my head was aching, and I told you that I wanted to go home."

Rose laughed disdainfully. "And do you expect me to believe that story?"

Cindy's eyes widened. "Why shouldn't you? It's the truth."

"Really!" Rose stopped laughing and drew herself up. "I'd thought that you might have come to your senses by now, but I can see that you haven't. I don't know

152

what you're trying to prove and I certainly don't intend to lose any sleep worrying about it. But neither do I intend to forget this!" With a toss of her head, she turned and walked away.

Cindy stared after her for a moment and then, sighing, went into the locker room. "And that's that," she thought. "Rose thinks I've let her down and she isn't ready to forgive me. I wish she didn't feel that way, but I suppose a split-up between us was inevitable. And if it had to happen, I'm glad it's happened now. The sooner Martha and the other girls see that I'm no longer going around with her, the easier it will be, probably, to make up with them."

Cindy's afternoon, however, was even more discouraging than her morning had been. Martha and Jan and Susan continued to avoid her, and after a while it began to seem to her that some of the other students were avoiding her, too—even those she barely knew. It became more and more difficult for her to keep smiling.

"It's worse than I thought it would be," she told herself. "So I'll just have to try that much harder. I'll have to meet everyone *more* than halfway."

At least she could detect no difference in Peter's manner. When she went to the library at four, he was working in his customary place at the long table, and the grin with which he greeted her was his usual friendly one.

"Hi, Cindy." He motioned her to a chair beside him.

"Glad you remembered to stop by. Several stories came in today."

Cindy sat down and glanced at the stack of papers on the table. The story on top of the pile, she saw, was a write-up of the junior prom.

"I was reading that just before you came in," Peter said. "Sounds like a nice affair."

"Yes, it was." Cindy turned to him curiously. "How come you weren't there?"

"Oh, I changed my mind and decided not to go." Suddenly Peter seemed to lose interest in the prom. He picked up the pile of stories and leafed through them. "Some of these need a good bit of work. No rush about it, though. They won't appear until the issue after next. But that story of yours will be in this time. Don't forget to look for it."

"I won't." Cindy had almost forgotten her telephone satire. Part of her purpose in writing it, she remembered, had been to impress the other students with her popularity. She wished now that she hadnt' tried to be so clever. "You don't happen to need another original story, do you!"

"I might. Why?"

"I'd like to try writing another. Maybe something a little more serious."

For a second Peter's expression was so odd that Cindy thought he'd misunderstood her. But then he said calmly, "Sure, go ahead," and she decided she'd been mistaken.

"I may not be able to use it immediately," he went on after a moment, "but it's always a good idea to have a backlog of material on hand. Any particular subject in mind?"

"No, nothing in particular," Cindy replied. "I want to think about it for a while."

Peter asked her when she thought she'd finish the rewrites, and she promised to turn them in on Friday. They talked for a few more minutes about the *Banner*, and Cindy kept hoping that he would say something about the Teen-Hi party at the Recreation Center, which she had heard was coming up again on Saturday night. But Peter didn't mention it.

It was still raining when she went outside and there was a strong wind which drove the rain in gusts under her umbrella, making it almost useless. "Talk about blue Monday!" she thought, pulling up the collar of her raincoat and shivering as she skirted a puddle at the foot of the steps. "For all that I accomplished today, I might as well have stayed home!"

But Monday was only the beginning of a long and lonely week for Cindy. Each morning, as she dressed for school, she told herself that today everything would be different. Today her schoolmates would smile when she smiled at them. Today they would decide that she had been punished long enough for her mistakes. But each afternoon, trudging home alone, she had to face the realization that she was getting nowhere in her attempt to make new friends. And the increasing talk about the forthcoming Teen-Hi night only served to emphasize her feeling of isolation.

At the Glee Club rehearsal Wednesday afternoon, she forced herself to make another overture to Martha and Jan and Susan.

"What about going down to Weyman's?" she asked, in as casual a voice as she could imagine. "I could stand a Coke and I imagine you," she looked at Susan, "are about ready for a sundae, aren't you?"

Susan refused to meet her eyes. "Why—uh—" she stammered, and looked at Martha.

Martha, coloring, glanced first at Susan and Jan and then at Cindy. "I'm sorry," she said, "but we weren't planning to go downtown today. I—I have some urgent things to take care of at home and so do Jan and Sue."

The excuse was so transparent that Cindy felt as though she'd been slapped. "Oh well . . . some other time then," she said lamely as Susan and Jan edged away.

"Yes, of course," Martha murmured, and hurried after the other girls.

Cindy couldn't understand it. Surely she had done nothing to deserve such a brush-off as this!

There was only one consolation. Sometime during the week, to Cindy's astonishment, Mack Gordon suddenly seemed to become aware of her. She wasn't sure exactly when it started, but one day, when she was sitting in study hall, she had a feeling that someone was watching her, and when she looked up, she found Mack

156

staring at her from his desk several aisles away. He caught her eye and nodded, but not in his usual careless way. He looked—Cindy searched her mind but there was no other word for it—*interested*.

And when the *Banner* came out Friday morning, Mack went out of his way to compliment her on her story, saying, "Clever piece of writing, Cindy. I'm beginning to think you're quite a girl!"

Cindy thanked him and turned away, as bewildered by Mack's sudden interest in her as by everything else that had happened this week. What had happened? Was Peter Holmes the only sane person left in Woodmont High?

When she took her rewrites to the school library at four, Peter also commented on her story. "It certainly attracted a lot of attention. I've been hearing about it all day and I suppose you have, too."

Ashamed to tell him that he and Mack were the only people who had mentioned the story to her, Cindy flushed and handed him the rewrites. "I think these are okay now. Anything else come in?"

Peter shook his head and brushed back his hair. "Not yet but I may have some more for you next week. How's the new story coming along?"

"What story?"

"The one you told me about last Monday."

"Oh." In the confusion and anxiety of the days since her last meeting with Peter, Cindy had forgotten her offer to write another story for the *Banner*. "I haven't started it yet," she admitted, "but I will as soon as I decide on a subject."

"I'll be looking forward to it," Peter said seriously. He told Cindy some of his plans for the next edition of the *Banner* and presently he said, "Well, that about winds it up for now. Drop around Monday or Tuesday, though, and I may have some more rewrites for you."

But he didn't invite her to the Teen-Hi night at the Rec.

CHAPTER

15

IT WAS RAINING AGAIN—a hard, driving rain that beat a steady rat-a-tat on the roof and splashed, gurgling, over the tops of the gutters. But Cindy neither saw nor heard the rain. Sitting beside the window in her darkened bedroom, she was thinking about the impasse which she seemed to have reached in Woodmont High.

Eleven days had passed since the junior prom but her daily, almost hourly, attempts to win new friends had produced negligible results. She had tried—oh, how she had tried, smiling constantly even when it hurt, and going out of her way to be pleasant and polite to everyone. But most of her fellow students were still ignoring her.

Their peculiar manner toward her was most noticeable between classes, when groups of students gathered together to talk. Each time Cindy approached one of these groups, it had a way of dissolving before her eyes. Yet she was sure that her classmates were aware of her; every now and then she would find one of them staring at her in an oddly speculative way, as though she were some sort of rare and unidentified laboratory specimen.

She couldn't understand it. It was true that her own behavior, both before and during the prom, had been questionable, but her intentions had been good. She had never deliberately done anything to hurt anyone. So why were they all deliberately hurting her now? She had expected to pay a penalty for her mistakes, but never such a severe one as this.

What had she done? Why was she being ostracized? Were they punishing her for ignoring them at the prom? And, if so, why had they made *her* the sole target of their disapproval? Rose and Mack and Bill had snubbed everyone at the dance, too, but no one seemed to be treating them differently from before. Of course Rose never had mingled much with the other students, and Mack and Bill were boys, after all, which might account for the fact that their actions were viewed with more tolerance.

Thinking of Mack, Cindy frowned at two raindrops which were tracing a course down the outside of the windowpane. Mack's behavior was another thing which mystified her. In sharp contrast to the other students, Mack was daily showing more and more interest in her. He was always watching her in class and in study hall, and lately he'd begun to stop her frequently between classes, to talk about some inconsequential thing or other. Yet it always happened when nobody else was near, as though he were reluctant to be seen with her. This increased Cindy's bewilderment.

What had she done? Why did so many people dislike her?

"Or am I imagining it?" she wondered, directing her gaze absently toward the slow-moving traffic on the wet street below. "I've always been too sensitive, so it's possible that I'm imagining a situation which doesn't exist at all, except in my mind. Maybe I've unconsciously been going around with a chip on my shoulder, looking for slights. Or maybe I've been trying too hard and pressing so much that I've frightened people away.

"But how could you make friends if you didn't try?"

Her mother made friends—literally dozens of them—without *seeming* to try. In the two months since moving to Woodmont, Mrs. Taylor had become active in church and welfare work. She went to the hospital one day each week and worked as a Gray Lady, and she had been on the committee for the latest blood bank drive. Scarcely a day passed that someone didn't call to ask for her help with one community project or another. And she was obviously well liked.

Suddenly Cindy rose from her seat beside the window, went to her bed, and stretched across it, her eyes thoughtful. Was that the secret? Hadn't she, Cindy, been *helpful* enough? Had she been thinking too much in terms of herself and not enough in terms of others?

"Maybe I have," she thought, chewing abstractedly on her thumbnail. "Maybe I've been self-centered without realizing it—so wrapped up in my own problems that I've been ignoring other people's problems. I wonder what would happen if I tried to be like Mother—if I forgot about myself and started looking for ways to help others. I might get a surprise. I might find everyone treating me entirely differently. It seems to work for Mother, so why shouldn't it work for me? At least it can't do any harm to try."

And, while she was looking for ways to be helpful, she could keep busy with schoolwork and with her work for the *Banner*. Yesterday Peter had given her three more rewrites to do and he'd asked her again about the new story she'd offered to write. Instead of lying here feeling sorry for herself, she ought to be working on the rewrites this very minute.

Seconds later, she was hard at work at the maple desk in the corner.

The Glee Club rehearsal the next afternoon was late in starting and, as Cindy took her place in the alto section, several of the girls around her were talking among themselves. Listening quietly to their conversation, she presently learned that half a dozen or so of them, including Martha and Jan and Susan, had taken up knitting as their latest pastime.

"None of us knows the first thing about it," Susan remarked, laughing, to the sophomore girl who sat be-

162

side her, in the seat directly behind Cindy's. "But we bought some yarn and needles and Martha found an instruction book in her attic. So we're all getting together at my house tonight to see what we can do."

"I wish I knew how to knit," the other girl said.

"Come on up if you'd like to try it," Susan told her. "I should warn you, though, that at the rate we're going, we'll be lucky if we ever finish one sweater among us."

Cindy's mother had taught her to knit two years ago, during an especially lonely summer. She had made a sweater for herself and a scarf for her father. "I could teach them," she thought wistfully. "At least I could teach them the beginning steps."

Then why not *offer* to teach them? Wasn't this exactly what she'd been looking for—an opportunity to be helpful?

She turned around and smiled at Susan. "I didn't mean to eavesdrop but I couldn't help overhearing what you said just now, and I thought you might be interested in knowing that I can knit."

"Is that so?" Susan's freckled face was expressionless.

"Yes, my mother taught me a couple of years ago. It's really not hard once you get the hang of it."

"I suppose not," Susan murmured. But she didn't invite Cindy to the get-together and, a moment later, she began to talk to the sophomore about something else.

Cindy's smile faded and the lump which formed in

her throat lasted all through the rehearsal, making it hard for her to sing.

But later, walking home alone, she told herself that she mustn't let one rebuff discourage her. Perhaps Susan had misinterpreted her remark and thought she was showing off. The next time she offered to help anyone, she must remember to choose her words more carefully and make sure that her motives were understood.

That night Cindy finished the rewrites Peter had given her to do and, with these out of the way, she could concentrate on the original story she had promised him. It took her a long time to choose a subject but she finally decided to write about a church service she had attended several years ago when she had camped with her mother and father at Cook Forest State Park in Pennsylvania.

The service had been held in a natural cathedral deep in the forest and it had been an informal affair, conducted by the campers themselves. But it had made a profound and lasting impression on Cindy. Even now she could remember how moved she had been as she sat on the ground gazing up at the tops of the pine trees and listening to the old, familiar hymns.

It was unlikely, she thought, that any of the Woodmont High students had ever had a similar experience, but she could share it with them if she could only get it on paper the way she had it in her mind. . . .

It was late by the time she finished the story, but

when she read over what she had written, she was well satisfied with her work. It wasn't a clever story, as her telephone story had been, but it was sincere.

And Peter liked it. He said so when she gave the story to him the next day. "Almost makes me feel as though I'd been there." He nodded approvingly at her from across the library table. "You've done a nice job, Cindy. This is the sort of writing I expected from you."

Cindy thanked him, and he said that if space permitted he'd try to work the story into the March 29th issue of the *Banner*. He went on to talk about some of his problems with the paper.

"Hey!" he said suddenly. "Don't you know that this is officially the first day of spring?"

Cindy started guiltily. While he'd been talking, her mind had drifted once again to her own problems. "So it is."

"Then why so glum? Don't you know that spring is supposed to be a happy time? A time when birds are singing and flowers are blooming and—" He interrupted himself to frown through the library window. "Though I'll have to admit that it doesn't look very springlike outside right now."

"No, it doesn't," Cindy agreed. Snow had been falling steadily all day and the drift on the window ledge was two inches deep.

"Well, in like a lion, out like a lamb," Peter said cheerfully.

Cindy grinned in spite of herself. "You're a little

mixed up. That's what they say about the first day of March, not the first day of spring." She paused, sobering. "But I'm sorry I tuned you out, Peter. I didn't mean to, but I have several things on my mind."

He gave her a quick, penetrating glance. "Anything I can do to help?"

Cindy hesitated, wondering if she dared confide in Peter. It would be a relief to tell her troubles to someone, and Peter was smart. He might be able to help her.

But how could she tell a boy—even as companionable a boy as Peter—something that she couldn't tell her parents? Besides, what if her problems turned out to be imaginary? After all, she didn't know for sure, did she?

"No, thanks," she said after a moment. "This is something I have to work out for myself."

"Well, let me know if you change your mind." Peter pushed back his hair with his habitual absent-minded gesture. "I can't have my number-one assistant going around in a blue fog indefinitely." He grinned. "It might interfere with your work!"

"I'll remember that," she said. "And someday maybe I will tell him about it," she thought, as she left the library. "Someday when it's all over and I can laugh."

During the following week, her spirits alternated constantly between hope and despair. At times, especially when she was having one of her increasingly frequent talks with Mack or when she was working with Peter on the newspaper, she told herself that she was worrying needlessly. Mack and Peter seemed to like her, so there couldn't be anything too desperate about her situation. The freeze she was getting from the other students was a temporary thing, emphasized out of all proportion by her own imagination. Someday, perhaps any day now, it would be over and forgotten.

But at other times she wasn't so confident. Hiding her inner disquiet behind an outward calm, she continued to be friendly and polite with everyone, and she watched constantly for ways to be helpful. But few such opportunities came along and, when they did, her suggestions and offers of help were invariably met with indifference. More than once, walking home alone at the end of the school day, she felt as though she'd been knocking her head against a stone wall.

But she couldn't give up. As long as there was any hope of improving her status in Woodmont High, she had to keep trying.

And then on Friday, March 29th—three weeks after the junior prom—something happened which left no further room for doubt in Cindy's mind.

The new *Banner* came out that morning and her story about the church service in the forest was featured on the first page, but no one commented to her about the story or even seemed to notice it. She tried not to mind, but she couldn't help feeling a little hurt.

When she went to the locker room after lunch to hang up her coat, she found Martha and several other girls there, talking about the Home Economics Club tea. This was an annual event, to be held this year during the third week in April, and traditionally the junior girls took care of the table decorations for the affair.

"I don't know," one of the girls was saying as Cindy joined them. "We could use spring flowers, I suppose."

"Or perhaps an Easter theme," said Martha, "with toy rabbits and baskets of colored eggs. I wish we could think of something more original, though. Doesn't anybody have any other suggestions?"

Cindy edged forward timidly. "What about an April showers theme? I saw it done one time in Exeter and it was lovely. The centerpieces were made of small, pastel-colord parasols, tied together and filled with flowers. And the parasols aren't hard to make; all it takes is some crepe paper and pipe cleaners. If you like the idea, I'll be glad to show you how to make them."

She glanced hopefully around the group, but everyone seemed to be looking the other way. The silence in the locker room was long and awkward.

It was ended finally by the heavy-set girl who was the secretary of the Home Economics Club. "I like Martha's idea about the Easter baskets better," she stated in a loud voice.

Several other girls promptly chimed in, agreeing with her, and there was a brief discussion about the best way to color Easter eggs. Nobody said a word about Cindy's idea.

Suddenly, staring at first one and then another of the chattering group of girls, Cindy was sure that they were ignoring the suggestion because it had come from

168

her. "They're acting as though they're afraid I'll contaminate them," she thought bewilderedly as the meeting broke up and some of the girls began to drift out.

Or was she imagining things again?

She had to know. She couldn't go on wondering forever.

Martha was halfway to the door. On a sudden impulse, Cindy drew her aside, out of the others' hearing. "Would you mind waiting for a minute, Martha?" she said quietly. "I want to ask you something."

"Is it important?" Martha glanced nervously at her watch. "I don't have much time."

"This won't take long. And I think it's important."

"Well . . . all right." Martha sat down on the end of the locker bench nearest the door. She seemed to be avoiding Cindy's eyes.

As soon as the others had gone, Cindy sat down beside her. "I'm sorry to detain you, Martha, but there's something I simply have to know." She took a deep breath to steady herself. "I can't help noticing that there's something peculiar about the way you and the other girls are treating me and—Well, what I wanted to ask you is, what's wrong? Have I done something to offend you?"

Martha's pink cheeks turned crimson. "Why, no, I can't imagine what ever gave you such an idea."

"I can't help thinking so when everybody keeps dodging me," Cindy said doggedly. "I must have done something you don't like." She hesitated. "Are you mad because of the way I acted at the prom? Because if you are, I want you to know that I'm very sorry about that."

"Oh, that's all right." Martha squirmed uncomfortably. "Nobody's given the prom another thought and you shouldn't either. Why don't you regard it as water over the dam and forget it?"

"But I can't forget it if it's made everyone mad at me!"

"Nobody's mad at you. I told you everybody's forgotten all about the prom." Martha turned suddenly as the locker-room door opened and Susan Greer poked her head around the corner.

"Oh, there you are, Martha!" cried Susan. "I've been looking all over for you. You'd better hurry if you're—" She caught sight of Cindy and her voice trailed away.

"I'm coming!" With obvious relief, Martha jumped to her feet. "Now don't worry, Cindy," she said hurriedly. "I'm sure everything will turn out all right." But her eyes still refused to meet Cindy's.

For a moment after the two girls had disappeared, Cindy continued to stare at the empty doorway. Then she wrenched her gaze away. The question in her mind had been answered. Even though Martha had admitted nothing, her evasiveness and embarrassment had revealed far more than she realized. Cindy was sure now that her rejection by her classmates hadn't been imagined. It was real.

But *why* had they rejected her? Martha had said that everyone had forgotten about the prom and, from the way she said it, Cindy believed her. But if it wasn't the prom, what was it? And how would Cindy ever find out if no one would tell her?

All at once the hurt and bewilderment swelled up from somewhere deep inside and she had to squeeze her eyes shut to keep from crying.

C H A P T E R

16

DISCOURAGED AND UNHAPPY, Cindy began to crawl into a shell. She no longer went out of her way to offer help, advice, or suggestions. What good would it do? How could she make people like her if she didn't know what it was that they *disliked* about her! It could be her appearance, her voice, anything! Maybe it was everything combined. Maybe she was so dull and unattractive and lacking in personality that she'd never had a chance of making friends in Woodmont.

She told herself that she didn't care—that if her classmates were determined to ignore her, she would simply ignore them, too. But even as she told herself these things, she knew that they weren't true. Cindy Taylor might pretend to be indifferent to others but she could never be indifferent to them in her heart.

And she couldn't shut herself away completely from

the life of Woodmont High. She had to go to school every day and attend her various classes. It became more and more difficult for her to keep her mind on her work, however, even in English III. Miss Ferguson spoke to her quite sharply, one day, for not paying attention in class.

"I'll simply have to snap out of it!" Cindy thought, red-faced with embarrassment. "If I don't, goodness only knows what will happen! I might even lose my job on the paper!"

But she couldn't seem to do it. When she went to the school library later that afternoon, Peter again commented on her obvious despondency.

"Sure you don't want to tell me what's bothering you?" he asked, leaning back in his chair and eying her thoughtfully. "Even if I can't help, it might make you feel better to get your troubles off your chest."

Once more, Cindy was tempted to confide in him; but she resisted the temptation. Any relief she might find in unloading her troubles on Peter could at best be only temporary. If people had decided that they didn't like her, what could *he* say or do to make them change their minds?

"Thanks, Peter." With an effort, she managed to make her voice light. "It's nice of you to offer but, as I told you before, this is something I have to work out for myself. Anyway, it really doesn't amount to much."

"Okay, if you don't want to tell me, I won't insist. But I think you're making a mistake. Don't you know that it's bad for your blood pressure to keep troubles bottled up too long?"

"There's nothing wrong with my blood pressure." Cindy attempted a laugh. "If it ever gets to the boiling point, I'll let you know, but it's nowhere near that point yet. Really it isn't."

Peter, however, didn't look entirely convinced.

That night, Cindy's mother again suggested inviting Sally Baird for a visit. "You and Sally were such close friends," she said, looking up from the kitchen table with a pencil poised above her uncompleted grocery list. "I know you must miss her and I'm sure Sally would love to come. Why don't you phone and invite her for next weekend? You could have a party for her Saturday night and introduce her to some of your Woodmont friends."

Cindy was standing at the sink, scraping the dinner plates. She turned on both faucets and let the water run noisily while she tried to think how she could answer her mother. She was still longing to see her old friend but now she had a new reason for not wanting Sally to come for a visit. It wouldn't take Sally any time at all to discover that Cindy had no friends in Woodmont.

"And Sally mustn't know," Cindy thought, stacking the plates carefully on the rubber dish mat. "I don't want Sally or anyone else ever to feel sorry for me." She turned off the faucets. "It's a nice idea, Mother, but I can't invite Sally just now. I—I'm too busy."

But her mother wasn't to be put off so easily. "Surely

you're not too busy to entertain an old friend, Lucinda. If the thought of a party worries you, I'll be happy to help. We'll keep the refreshments simple—perhaps have a buffet."

Cindy hesitated, wondering what she could offer as an excuse. And suddenly she thought, "Why make excuses? I can't hide the truth from Mother and Dad forever. They're bound to know the real state of affairs sooner or later." She swung around and faced her mother. "It's not the refreshments I'm worried about. The reason I don't want to have a party is that I don't know anyone to invite."

Her mother looked startled. "What about the girls you've been telling me about—the ones who are in the Glee Club with you? Wouldn't you like to invite them? Or Mack and the couple who went with you to the prom?"

"I don't know any of them well enough to invite them to a party!"—"And if I did invite them," Cindy thought, "they wouldn't come." She made herself go on. "You might as well know how it is, Mother. Even though we've been living here for more than two months now, I haven't made any friends!"

The surprise in her mother's face gave way to a look of concern. "You must be exaggerating, Cindy. Perhaps you haven't yet made any close friends here, but I'm sure you will in time."

"Will I?" All at once Cindy had to blink to hold back the tears. "'You're forgetting something, Mother. I'm just not the kind of person who attracts other people. I—I'm sorry to be such a disappointment to you and Dad but that's the way it is!"

"A disappointment? Oh, no, Cindy." Her mother got up, crossed the room, and put her hands on Cindy's shoulders, gazing earnestly into her eyes. "Your father and I are very proud of you, don't you know that? We're proud of the way you look, the fine grades you make in school, your work on the newspaper—everything you do."

There was no mistaking her sincerity.

"But you'll have to admit I'm not popular!" Cindy blurted.

Mrs. Taylor shook her head. "I don't admit any such thing. It's my guess that you're better liked than you think. And I also predict that some of your new classmates will eventually become very good friends of yours." She gave Cindy's shoulders an affectionate squeeze and returned to the table. "In the meantime, if I were you, I'd try not to worry about it. Just be yourself and let friendships develop naturally. If you prefer, we'll postpone having Sally down for a while. But remember, the best way to have a friend is to *be* one."

"Well, I'll try," Cindy said. But she couldn't help sighing as she turned back to the sink. "Mother just doesn't understand," she thought to herself. "What she doesn't know is that I've already tried everything in the book—and failed!"

The very next day, however, Cindy changed her mind. She was returning to the school after lunch when Mack Gordon suddenly broke away from a group of boys standing near the entrance. "Hey, wait a minute, Cindy," he called. "I want to talk to you."

Cindy turned and waited, wondering what he wanted to talk about this time. Mack's conversations with her were getting to be an almost daily occurrence but he never seemed to have anything important to say.

As he strolled up to her now, however, she noticed immediately that there was something different about his expression. She couldn't define it exactly, but it was as though his new awareness of her had sharpened and come into focus.

"Where did you go after school yesterday?" he asked. "I looked around for you but couldn't find you."

"You did?"

"Yes, I was going to give you a lift home."

Cindy didn't know whether to believe him or not. "I was in the library," she explained. "Had some *Banner* material to turn in to Peter." Smiling uncertainly, she started on down the corridor.

Mack swung into step beside her. "That's right, I keep forgetting you're a newspaper gal. I couldn't do it in a month of Sundays."

"Do what?"

"Write the kind of stuff you've been turning out for the *Banner*."

"Oh, I don't know." Cindy could feel him looking

down at her. She fastened her own eyes on the gym door at the end of the corridor. "You probably could if you wanted to."

"Not me. Never let it be said that I don't know my own limitations." Mack was silent for a moment. "What beats me is how a girl as cute as you are can do it. I always thought that pretty girls were naturally short on brains. Now here you are, knocking my pet theory into a cocked hat!"

Was he making fun of her? Cindy couldn't tell from his voice and she was too flustered to look at him. She began to walk a little faster.

But Mack kept pace with her. "Are you doing anything tomorrow night?" he asked suddenly.

The question startled Cindy so much that she almost stumbled. What was he leading up to? Could it possibly be what it sounded like? She ventured an upward glance, but Mack's expression was inscrutable. "Why, no," she replied carefully.

"I thought that if you weren't going to be busy, we might go out somewhere," he said calmly. "Take in a dance or a show or something."

Cindy stared at him, scarcely daring to believe her ears. Entirely of his own accord, without prompting from Rose or anyone, Mack was asking her for a date!

"Don't look so surprised," he said. "I've been wanting to take you out for a long time, but didn't have a car. Dad got sore over the late hours I was keeping and took the station wagon keys away from me, the day after the

178

prom. I didn't get them back until yesterday." He grinned at her lazily. "Well, is it yes or no?"

It took all of the poise she could muster to keep her voice from shaking. "Why, yes, I think I can make it. What time?"

"Suppose I come up for you around eight-thirty. Okay?"

"Okay."

They reached the door of the girls' locker room, and parted. But, for several seconds after the locker-room door had closed behind her, Cindy stood leaning against it, too dazed to move.

Her spirits were soaring, not only in anticipation of another date with Mack but because of what his invitation signified. "A prominent boy like Mack," she told herself, "would never date a girl who was generally disliked"; therefore she must have been mistaken in thinking she had been rejected. She had exaggerated a few minor, and probably accidental, slights and had allowed them to build up in her mind until they'd achieved an importance out of all proportion to their true importance.

But at least she had learned her lesson and would never make the same mistake again. From now on, she would do as her mother had advised: be herself and let friendships develop naturally. All that was needed was time.

C H A P T E R

17

So far, everything was going smoothly, Cindy thought. Even the weather seemed to be cooperating. The night was cold but clear, with hundreds of stars twinkling in the sky, and when she leaned forward and peered up to the right, she could see a pale yellow sliver of moon shining through a corner of the station wagon windshield.

Mack had been a little late in calling for her and he hadn't seemed to want to spend much time visiting with her parents, but Cindy thought she understood why. If he intended to take her dancing somewhere, he'd probably be in a hurry to start because most of the dancing spots around Woodmont closed at twelve o'clock on Saturday nights.

He was still in a hurry. Slouched in the driver's seat, with his finger tips resting lightly on the steering wheel, he was weaving the station wagon in and out of downtown traffic at a speed that was much too fast for safety. But, remembering how annoyed he'd been with her on the night of the prom, Cindy was determined not to say anything, no matter how fast he drove.

As he eased the car out onto the highway, she stole a surreptitious glance at him. The road they were taking was the one which went past Gorley's. Was it possible that Mack intended to take her there? It would be wonderful if he did. Some of the other Woodmont High students would be sure to be there and see her with him. Of course, the other time they'd gone to Gorley's, Mack had said that he didn't like the place. But maybe he hadn't meant it. Maybe he, too, had been putting on an act for the benefit of Rose and Bill.

Mack turned his head unexpectedly and caught her glance. He laughed softly. "Penny for your thoughts."

"Oh, nothing. I was just thinking about what a nice night it is." Embarrassed, Cindy transferred her gaze to the dashboard.

"Yes." Mack swung the car around another, slower, one and his foot eased up slightly on the throttle. "A lot nicer than the last time we were out together. Too bad you didn't go on to the Eagles' Nest with us that night. I suppose Rose told you that we didn't get home till four in the morning."

"No. As a matter of fact Rose hasn't said much of anything to me since then. I guess she's still peeved because I didn't go with you."

181

"That's Rose! She has quite a temper and she shows it sometimes when she doesn't get her own way. But don't worry, she'll get over it." He laughed again. "The family heard me coming in at four and raised Cain about it. That's why Dad took away the car keys. I told them that you'd made me take you home early, though, so your stock's still high."

Cindy was silent, wondering if Mack remembered that he, too, had been angry with her that night. "Better not remind him," she thought. "If he does remember, he's probably sorry and it would only embarrass him if I mentioned it now." Turning, she glanced through the window. There wasn't much to see—just the dark, shadowy forms of the trees along the side of the road and an occasional cluster of lights as a farmhouse or gas station flashed by.

"I'm actually having a date with Mack Gordon," she thought wonderingly. "And I didn't have to hint to Rose or anyone."

It still seemed almost unbelievable, but it was happening. There was the excited beating of her heart to prove it and, for added proof, when she turned her head a little, there was Mack himself, sitting only a few inches away. How handsome he was! Even in the dark, his hair had a faint gleam, as though reflecting the light of those hundreds of stars overhead.

He glanced at her again. "How do you like living in Woodmont by now?"

"Oh, fine." Cindy hesitated and decided that there

182

was no point in trying to conceal the truth from him. "It does seem like a rather hard place to get acquainted, though."

Mack nodded. "It probably seems dull to you now, but give it time. You'll find plenty to do once you know your way around."

"I hope so."

They were both silent again. Presently Mack switched on the radio and, as the sound of soft dance music filled the air, Cindy began to wonder once more about their destination. If Mack intended to take her to Gorley's she would soon be in his arms, dancing to just such music as this. There . . . she could see Gorley's electric sign glowing in the darkness up ahead. In a flurry of anticipation, she patted her hair and began to pull on her gloves.

But when they were opposite Gorley's, Mack kept on going without slowing down or showing the slightest inclination to turn into the driveway. Cindy told herself that it was ridiculous to be disappointed. She shouldn't have assumed that he meant to take her to Gorley's. Probably he had an even nicer place in mind, perhaps some place in the city where they had a real orchestra instead of a jukebox for dancing.

Mack, however, didn't stop in the city. He drove all the way through town to the eastern suburbs and kept on going. When he finally did turn off the road, it was to pull into a drive-in theater about three miles beyond the outskirts of the city, and he didn't bother to ask

Cindy whether or not she wanted to see the show. He bought their tickets and drove on in and parked, and all that he said was, "Want some popcorn or a Coke or anything?"

"No, thanks," Cindy replied. She tried to hide her disappointment but it was there. And, to add to her feeling of letdown, the movie turned out to be one she had already seen—a murder mystery that had been interesting the first time, but not the second.

Mack seemed to be enjoying it, however, so for his sake she pretended to be as absorbed in the movies as he was, even when, after a while, he slid his arm around the back of the seat so that his hand was resting lightly on her shoulder.

She was sure that it was an unconscious gesture rather than a deliberate one. But after that she was so aware of Mack's presence beside her that she couldn't possibly have followed the plot of the movie, so it was probably just as well that it was one she had already seen.

When they came out of the drive-in, Mack surprised her again by turning the car to the left, away from the direction they had come. She wanted to ask him where they were going, but he was so quiet and the look on his face was so remote that she lacked the courage.

They had gone five miles beyond the drive-in before he broke the silence. "You're not in any hurry to go home, are you? I thought we might ride around for a while."

According to the clock on the dashboard it was five after twelve—high time for Cindy to be starting home. But, afraid of displeasing Mack, she swallowed her misgivings. "Just so it isn't too long a ride."

"It won't be," he said obscurely.

He drove for another ten minutes along the highway and finally turned off into a country lane, so dark and narrow that it was hard to believe that it led anywhere except to some farmer's pasture. It must be a short-cut, Cindy thought. Maybe it's a short cut back to Woodmont. But she began to feel uneasy. It was so dark here and Mack was so quiet.

They bumped along the rough, rutted road in silence for another two miles. Then suddenly Mack pulled the station wagon off into a small clearing beside the road and shut off the motor. Without a word, he pulled Cindy over to him and gave her a long kiss.

Cindy was so startled that for a moment she was limp in his arms. She had dreamed of being kissed by Mack. But not—not like this! All at once, appalled, she pulled away from him.

"What's the big idea?" he demanded angrily.

"That's what I'd like to know," she retorted.

He drew a pack of cigarettes from his pocket and lit one. In the glow from the match, she saw that he was scowling. He threw away the match. "What did you expect?"

"I—I don't know what you mean." Cindy's hands

185

were beginning to tremble. She clenched them tightly together.

"Oh, no?" Mack took a long draw on his cigarette and a thin spiral of smoke winged its way toward the roof of the car. "What kind of a line are you trying to hand me? You, with your oh-so-pure-and-noble story about a church service in the forest! Who do you think you're kidding? I know your kind. I wasn't born yesterday."

"Wh—what do you mean, you know my kind?"

"I know what you were like before you moved here. Rose inquired about you the weekend she visited that friend of hers who lives near your old home town, and her friend knew the whole story. She told Rose, and Rose told Bill and me the night of the prom, after I took you home."

"The whole story?" Cindy echoed bewilderedly. "What story?"

"That's why Rose is so burned up at you," Mack continued, "and I can't say that I blame her. This 'little Miss Innocent' routine of yours is hard to take when we know the kind of a stunt you pulled in Exeter. What beats me is how you thought you could keep it a secret. You should have known that we'd hear about it sooner or later."

"You'd hear about what?" Cindy's voice was high and strained. "I don't know what you're talking about!"

"Oh, no?" Mack laughed sarcastically. "Allow me to refresh your memory. I'm referring to the time you

186

tried to elope with some college boy and lied about your age in order to get a license! Too bad your boy friend smashed up his car and another one, and tried to get away from the scene of the accident before you got to the justice of the peace. It must have been quite a mess when the cops discovered you were trying to elope. Tell me, did you spend much time in jail before your parents came and bailed you out?"

Cindy was so stunned that it took her a minute to find her voice. "But that's not true! I never did anything like that in my life! I can't imagine what made Rose and her friend say—" She broke off, catching her lower lip between her teeth. There *had* been such a scandal in Exeter, three years ago, while she was still in junior high. The girl involved had been a high school senior—a very pretty girl named Cynthia Blakeslee, and the attempted elopement had been the talk of Exeter for weeks after it happened. Eventually Cynthia and her family had moved away from Exeter and the talk had died down. Until this minute, Cindy had all but forgotten the story.

"Well?" said Mack.

Cindy let out her breath in a long, deep sigh. "Something like that did happen when I lived in Exeter, Mack, but not to me. The girl was an older girl named Cynthia and I didn't even know her very well. But our first names are similar; I guess that must be why Rose and her friend confused Cynthia with me. They shouldn't have repeated the story, though, without being sure of their facts." All at once a new and frightening thought came into Cindy's mind. "Mack, tell me something, please! How many other people in Woodmont High have heard this story about me?"

"Probably most of them by now. What's the difference?"

"What's the difference?" Cindy repeated incredulously. She thought of her unhappiness in recent weeks —of the heartbreak she had suffered over her lack of friends. So her rejection hadn't been imaginary, after all! She *had* been repudiated, because of malicious and completely unfounded gossip!

"What's the difference?" she said again in a small, aching whisper. "Don't you know how it makes me feel to know that people have been gossiping about me?"

"What can you do about it? I told you it was bound to come out sooner or later." Mack rolled down a window and tossed out his cigarette. "Let 'em talk!"

"But what they're saying about me isn't true!"

"Don't give me that!" Mack's tone was flat and cold. "You don't think I believe that little story you cooked up about a girl with a name like yours, do you? What kind of a fool do you think I am?"

Cindy heard his words and strangely, for just a second, her mind refused to accept them. "He couldn't have said what I thought he did," she told herself dazedly. "Not Mack."

Then comprehension sank in and, simultaneously,

her world came crashing down around her ears. Mack didn't believe her. She had told him the truth but he thought she was lying. And this was the boy she liked better than any she had ever known!

A lump formed in her throat but she was determined not to let him see how much he had hurt her. Straightening, she moved over against the door, as far away from him as possible. "I want to go home, Mack," she said quietly. "Please take me home."

Mack stared at her, then abruptly turned on the ignition. But he couldn't resist one final thrust. "Okay," he said grimly, as he backed the station wagon around. "If you insist on being coy, I'm darned if I'm going to argue with you. But don't get the notion that I've fallen for this routine of yours. It'll be a long, cold day before I ask you for a date again, believe me!"

The long ride home was made in total silence.

C H A P T E R

18

Cindy had always hated gossip. In Exeter, she had made it a rule never to repeat any for, as she had often said to Sally, "It seems so underhanded, somehow, to talk about people when they aren't around to defend themselves."

Now she herself was the victim of gossip. Could she have defended herself if she had known what people were saying? What could she do about it now?

For hours after she had gone to bed, she lay awake reliving the scene with Mack, hearing again his cold, cutting words: *I know what you were like before you moved here. . . . Rose told Bill and me the night of the prom. . . .*

And then the story—the dreadful, damaging story of a girl whose elopement had been thwarted by the police. How many other Woodmont High students had heard and repeated it? Probably most of them, Mack had said, and Cindy had no reason to doubt him. They had been whispering about her and laughing at her behind her back ever since the night of the prom. She could imagine what they'd been saying:

Have you heard about that new girl, Cindy Taylor?
No, what about her?
Wait till I tell you about the scrape she was in before she came to Woodmont!

The story must have spread like wildfire. Such stories usually did. Mack had said that her stock was still high with his family, so apparently the talk had been confined to the high school students, so far. But sooner or later it was bound to spread among their parents, too. And then it would be only a question of time until it came to the ears of Cindy's mother and father.

What would they say? What would they do?

"They'll be angry and embarrassed about the lies," Cindy thought apprehensively. "And they'll be terribly ashamed of me when they find out that my behavior has made the lies credible."

She could see it only too clearly now. Nobody in Exeter would ever have believed such a story about "Beanpole" Taylor, but here in Woodmont, where she was unknown, why shouldn't they believe it? Cindy had worked hard to give a false impression of herself. Looking back, she could see that almost everything she had done was open to misinterpretation. Her vagueness about her life in Exeter could easily have seemed like an attempt to conceal her "past." Her preference for Rose's company could have been interpreted as a natural desire to be with someone of her own kind.

Why had Rose deliberately started the story? "Probably to get even," Cindy thought, tossing restlessly from one side of her bed to the other. "Rose was pretty mad that night when I wouldn't go on to the Eagles' Nest, and I can understand why now, if she'd heard this story about me and believed it. She probably thought I was being inconsistent. Even so, though, she shouldn't have talked about me without being sure of her facts."

But Rose *had* talked and the talk had spread all over school. No wonder Cindy had found the going so rough. No wonder she hadn't made any friends, with the possible exception of Peter Holmes.

What about Peter? Why had he, alone among Cindy's schoolmates, continued to be friendly to her? It must be that Peter had somehow missed hearing the gossip, perhaps because he was usually so immersed in his newspaper work that he didn't have much time to talk with the other kids. But he would hear it eventually and, when he did—

It wasn't fair! People had no right to criticize someone they didn't even know! At the very least, they should have given her a chance to explain.

"But what can I do?" Cindy asked herself despairingly. "It won't do any good to deny the story. If Mack wouldn't believe me, who will?"

What could she do? The question was still unanswered when she finally fell into a troubled sleep.

School, for Cindy, became an ordeal—a routine which had to be endured but which she approached daily with a feeling of dread. And always, each day, the worst moment was when she had to walk into her home room and face her classmates, knowing that they had gossiped about her, knowing that they might even now be speculating among themselves about her. Once again she deliberately assumed an air of indifference, hiding her distress behind a mask of cold disdain. She never smiled and she spoke only when someone spoke to her. And if, at times, she was tempted to break down, pride kept her going. No matter what happened, she mustn't let anyone see how much she had been hurt!

She decided to concentrate all of her time and attention on her schoolwork, and the newspaper assignments. "From now on," she resolved grimly, "I won't even think about other people. Let them say whatever they want to say about me. I simply won't care."

But Cindy soon discovered that the resolution which had sounded so noble in theory wasn't easy to carry out in practice. A schedule composed entirely of working, eating, and sleeping left unfilled gaps in her life, and there were times when she couldn't escape the knowledge that she was desperately unhappy.

Thursday afternoon, with her lesson assignments completed for the rest of the week, she was suddenly unable to face the thought of another lonely evening. "I'll run up to the library and see if Peter has any rewrites for me," she thought. "He probably *won't* have, with the new issue coming out tomorrow. But something may have been turned in early.

When she reached the library it was empty but, as she was turning away, Peter came up the stairs, his arms filled with the usual assortment of books and papers.

"Hi, Cindy." As always, his grin seemed genuinely friendly. "Looking for me?"

"Yes, I wondered if you had any rewrites for me."

"No, not yet." He halted at the top of the steps.

"Oh. Well, let me know when something comes in." Disappointed, Cindy started past him but he stopped her.

"If you're not in any hurry, why not stick around for a while. We haven't had much chance to talk lately."

"Well . . . all right." Glad to postpone her solitary walk home, Cindy returned to the library with him and took her usual place at the table.

Peter dumped his books and papers on the table and sat down beside her, brushing back his hair. "Seems as though this newspaper business is either all feast or all famine," he remarked. "Either we're up to our ears in work or we're sitting around wondering what to do to put in the time."

"So it seems," Cindy murmured stiffly.

There was a sudden silence.

All at once Peter slammed one fist down on the table. "Okay," he said gruffly. "Let's have it!"

Startled, Cindy blinked at him. "Let's have what?"

"Whatever it is that's on your mind." Peter gave her a long, searching look. "For almost a month now, you've been going around in a fog, looking as though you were carrying the weight of the world on your shoulders, and I've had all I can take of it. You might as well make up your mind to tell me what's wrong, Cindy. You're going to sit here until you do."

"There's nothing wrong."

"Let's not go through all that again. You've been holding out on me entirely too long as it is. Come on, let's have it!"

"But I can't tell you! Even if I did, it wouldn't help. You wouldn't believe me!"

"Why not try me and see?"

"But I can't! It wouldn't do any good and I—I " At a loss for words, Cindy stammered to a halt and stared at Peter mutely. And then, to her horror, she broke down. It started with a trembling in her knees that spread to her arms and shoulders, and suddenly she burst into tears. She covered her face with her hands.

She cried for several minutes. When her sobs finally

began to diminish, Peter thrust his handkerchief into her hands. "Here, use this."

She wiped her eyes and blew her nose. "I'm sorry. I don't know what came over me."

"I do. You reached that boiling point we were talking about—and something had to give." Leaning back in his chair, Peter calmly crossed his knees and folded his arms across his chest. "Feel better now?"

Cindy nodded.

"Then suppose you tell me what this is all about."

For some reason, his quiet words caused a fresh lump to form in Cindy's throat. "I—I can't," she repeated, swallowing.

There was another silence. "All right," Peter said after a moment, "if you can't—or won't—tell me, suppose I guess. Does it have anything to do with Mack Gordon?"

Cindy couldn't deny it, not with Peter's eyes gazing so candidly into her own. "In a way, yes. At least Mack brought things to a head. I had a date with him last Saturday but—" her voice broke slightly, "but it wasn't the kind of date I thought it was going to be."

"I see." Peter's mouth tightened. "Gordon!" he muttered angrily. "For two cents, I'd hunt him up right now and tell him what I think of him!"

"No!" Strangely, even after all that had happened, Cindy still felt impelled to defend Mack. "It's not his fault—at least not entirely. You can't blame him for believing what everybody else believes."

"What do you mean?"

"You haven't heard the gossip?"

"What gossip?"

"About me." Cindy flushed, clasped her hands together, and made herself go on. "There's a story going around that I tried to elope with a college boy when I was living in Exeter. They say that I—I lied about my age in order to get a marriage license and that we wrecked the car on our way to the justice of the peace. When the police learned that we were trying to elope, they stopped us, of course." She tilted her chin defiantly. "It's quite a scandal! I'm surprised you haven't heard it."

"Well, I haven't." Peter's voice was matter-of-fact. "Even if I had, I'd never have believed it."

"You wouldn't?"

"Of course not. Nobody could know you and believe a story like that about you."

Peter didn't believe the gossip even though she hadn't denied it! Cindy stared at him wonderingly for a minute, then slowly shook her head. "You're wrong. Almost everybody *does* believe it, including Mack. He told me so Saturday night."

"He would!" Again Peter's mouth tightened at the corners. "But if I were you, I wouldn't take Mack's opinion as a criterion of what other people are thinking." He frowned. "What I can't understand is how a farfetched story like that happened to get started."

"It's not so farfetched. There *was* a scandal like that

197

in Exeter." Cindy told him about Cynthia Blakeslee and about her belief that it was the similarity in names which had led to Rose's garbling of the facts.

"And you explained this to Mack Saturday night?" Peter asked when she had finished.

"Yes, but he didn't believe me." Cindy swallowed again, remembering. "But at least I know now why the other kids have been treating me the way they do." She told Peter about the freeze she had been getting from most of the students. "So you see," she concluded, "in a way I'm glad it came out, even though there's nothing I can do about it."

"What do you mean—nothing you can do about it?" Peter's tone was suddenly sharp. "You aren't going to take a thing like this lying down, are you?"

"What else can I do? I can't go around making wholesale denials when nobody but Mack has openly accused me of anything, can I? Besides, nobody would believe me if I did. Nobody here really knows me— except you, perhaps, through my work on the paper." Cindy hesitated, biting her lower lip. "If you must know, most of the kids had the wrong impression of me anyway, long before the gossip started. I deliberately *gave* them the wrong impression."

"How so?" Peter asked quietly.

She took a deep breath. "You might as well know everything, Peter. I—I'm not the kind of girl—well, I'm not what I seem to be. I'm awkward and shy, and back in Exeter I wasn't very popular. So, when we moved here, I purposely put on an act because I was hoping to—hoping to—"

"I understand." To Cindy's relief, Peter looked neither amused nor particularly shocked by her admission. His eyes reflected only concern. "But thanks for telling me, Cindy." Suddenly he rose and went to the window, where he stood looking out for several seconds, his back to Cindy. When he turned around, he was frowning again. "But I still think something should be done to set everybody straight where you're concerned."

"But what can I do?"

"I think you ought to have it out with Rose. Make her admit that she started the story about you without knowing the facts. If possible, make her promise to tell everyone the truth at once."

"Have it out with Rose!" Cindy repeated. She thought of Rose's haughty eyes, her arrogance, her disdainful laugh. "I couldn't do anything like that, Peter. I'd never have nerve enough to stand up to her and make her admit that she was wrong. I just told you—I'm not the brave, bold person I've been pretending to be. I—I've always been more the timid mouse type."

"Then I think it's time for you to get over it." Peter returned to the table and sat down again, facing her. "Seriously, Cindy, I think it's the only thing to do. I could go around and talk to some of the kids, of course, and I will if it comes to that. But anything I say is

199

bound to be offset to a certain extent as long as Rose continues to gossip about you. And the only way to stop Rose, as I see it, is for you to face up to her. Maybe you won't be able to make her back down, but you should try—for the sake of your morale, if nothing else. Won't you give it a try?"

"But words that have been said can't be unsaid," Cindy reminded him unhappily.

"We'll see about that," said Peter.

CHAPTER

19

For four days Cindy thought about Peter's advice, mentally debating its pros and cons, without being able to come to a decision. Her mind told her that Peter's arguments were sound and that a showdown with Rose was the only sensible solution to her problem; yet she shied away from the thought of confronting Rose. To do so would unquestionably mean a scene, and Cindy had always avoided scenes. "Besides," she told herself frequently, "it probably wouldn't accomplish a thing. Before we were through, Rose would probably have me convinced that *I* was wrong."

As it turned out, Miss Ferguson was indirectly responsible for bringing matters to a head. The English teacher kept Cindy after school, Monday, to talk about the possibility of forming a writing club in Woodmont High, and it took her fifteen minutes to outline her ideas. When Cindy finally left the room and went to get her coat, the building was almost empty and the corridors were deserted.

To save time, she decided to use the rear exit. She had reached the end of the corridor and was passing the gymnasium when she heard a faint sound behind her and, glancing back, saw Rose come out of one of the classrooms.

Rose was looking the other way, and Cindy's first inclination was to pretend that she hadn't seen her. But suddenly, as she hesitated, she thought, "Why not have it out with her now, when nobody else is around? I'll never find a better time, so it's now or never.—"

"Rose!" she called impulsively. "Can you come here for a minute?"

Rose turned. "Oh, it's you!" She came walking back toward Cindy, her heels clicking loudly in the silence of the empty corridor.

As she approached, Cindy drew back involuntarily into the doorway of the darkened gym. Rose's expression was aloof, her bearing haughty. Obviously she had lost none of her recent hostility.

She halted and her eyes met Cindy's with icy indifference. "What's on your mind?"

"I—I—" Cindy paused, unnerved by the other girl's manner. "How come you're so late today?"

"I had a Latin test to make up. Why?"

"Oh, I just wondered." Cindy hesitated again, wondering how she could possibly say what *had* to be said.

202

For a moment, she was tempted to give up, to invent an excuse for calling to Rose, and let it go at that. "But if I do," she thought, "I'll never, never get up enough nerve to try again." She braced herself. "I do have something to say to you, Rose. Ever since the junior prom, I've been getting the cold shoulder from almost everyone in school. I didn't know what was wrong until recently, when I discovered that I've been the victim of some pretty malicious gossip. And, according to my information, you are the one who started it."

"Really?" Rose's face was the picture of innocence. "I haven't the faintest idea what you're talking about."

Cindy's reaction to the bland denial was swift and unexpected. For just a second, she stared speechlessly at Rose. Then, all at once, she became angry.

"I think you do, Rose," she said, in a voice completely unlike any she had ever used before. This wasn't the cool Cindy Taylor speaking—nor was it the timid "Beanpole" of Exeter. This was a new Lucinda Taylor, filled with righteous indignation and, to her own amazement, unafraid. "I'm referring to that wild story you've been telling about my so-called attempted elopement. I had a date with Mack a week ago last Saturday night and he told me all about it. He also told me that you started the story, so there's no use trying to deny it."

"Oh, that." Rose, too, seemed amazed by Cindy's sudden outburst. Her face lost its look of innocence and she glanced quickly around the corridor. Her eyes returned to Cindy and she colored slightly. "What if I did? You certainly didn't think you were going to keep it a secret forever, did you?"

"But it's not true! I was never involved in anything like that—in Exeter or any place else!"

"That's not the way I heard it! You forget, Cindy, I have a friend who lives near Exeter. She told me the entire story that weekend I visited her and, believe me, she didn't omit any of the lurid details."

"Did she mention any dates?"

"Well, no, I don't believe she did."

"That's what I thought." Cindy's indignation mounted. "There *was* a scandal like that in Exeter, but it happened several years ago, when I was still in junior high. The girl involved was a high school senior and she happened to have a first name similar to mine, but that's the only similarity between us. I was only thirteen years old at the time she tried to elope. So, don't you see, it couldn't have been me? If your friend said that it was, she was either guessing or lying!"

"Well," Rose's glance wavered, "now that I think about it, she didn't say that she was positive it was you. But she *thought* you were the girl she'd heard about."

"And you passed the story along without being sure?"

"Well, yes." Rose looked a little sheepish. She shifted her weight from one foot to the other. Then, abruptly, she began to laugh. "But what do you care? I gather that the talk's aroused Mack's interest in you, since he

204

asked you for a date. And that's what you wanted, isn't it?"

The last thing Cindy had expected was laughter. "But I *should* have expected it," she thought. "I should have known that if I pinned Rose down she'd try to make light of everything. It's right in character."

She clenched her hands in a fresh spurt of anger. "But I do care, Rose. I've been worried sick ever since I found out what was going on. And I hoped you'd be willing to do something about it, once you learned the truth."

"Do something about it? What could I do?"

"You could tell everyone that you've learned you were wrong about me. People would listen to you since you're the one who started the gossip."

"Are you kidding?" Rose laughed again, disdainfully.

"You mean you won't do it, even knowing how much it means to me?"

"I certainly won't."

"Oh yes, you will!"

Cindy and Rose turned simultaneously. The gym door was open and Mack Gordon was standing there, not more than a foot away from them.

"Where did you come from?" gasped Rose.

Mack's eyes flicked over her coldly. "From the gym; where else?"

"How long have you been in there?"

"Long enough." Mack turned to Cindy. "I forgot my sweat shirt and had to come back for it. I was on my way out again when I happened to hear you out here and decided to tune in. Good thing I did. It was quite an earful. I never knew you had so much spunk!"

Cindy gulped. "Then you heard—?"

"Every word. I was standing just inside the door and it isn't soundproof." He turned back to Rose. "About this gossip you've been spreading around, why didn't you say that you weren't sure Cindy was the girl involved? Or, better yet, why didn't you keep your mouth shut?"

"Oh, for Heaven's sake, Mack, why all the fuss?" For the first time since Cindy had known her, Rose seemed to have lost some of her poise. Her face had paled and she was talking faster than usual. "People are always gossiping about someone. What difference does it make who happens to be the latest target?"

"I think it makes quite a difference," Mack said sternly. "It's one thing if the gossip has some basis in fact, another thing if it's based on hearsay. It hadn't occurred to me that we might have figured wrong about Cindy. But you wouldn't understand that, Rose." He gave her a long, level look. "The thing is, what do you intend to do about it?"

"Do about it?"

"Are you going to do as Cindy asked and tell everyone that you were wrong about her? Or do I have to do it for you?"

"Why, of course, Mack." Rose's lashes fluttered upward and she tried to smile. "I never intended to cause

Cindy any trouble; surely you know me well enough to know that. But if you think I have, I'll be glad to do anything I can to—"

"You can skip the hearts and flowers," Mack cut in harshly. "Just see to it that you put a stop to the gossip, and the sooner the better."

"Of *course!*" Rose repeated. She glanced at Cindy, took a hesitant step forward, and placed a conciliatory hand on Mack's arm. "And now that that's settled, can't we talk about something else for a change? I know what!" She smiled again, placatingly. "If you're driving your station wagon this afternoon, why don't we find Bill and all take a ride somewhere?"

"Sorry." Mack brushed off her hand as though he were brushing away a troublesome fly. "I have some things to talk over with Cindy privately."

"Oh." Rose's hand fell to her side and she gazed at him uncertainly for a second, then her customary aplomb reasserted itself and she tossed her head. "Well, if that's the way it is, I'll run along then. Be seeing you!" She flashed another smile, waved, and was gone.

"What a performance!" said Mack. He looked at Cindy and there was a sudden, strained silence. He cleared his throat. "Knowing Rose, though, I'm not sure we can depend on her, so I think I'll talk to a few people myself—just to make sure that nobody has any wrong ideas about you." A slow red flush crept over his neck and ears. "And, speaking of wrong ideas, Cindy, I guess I had a few of them, too. About that date we had, I—I—" he broke off, obviously hoping for an interruption.

Cindy was silent. "It's up to him," she thought.

He pulled out a handkerchief and mopped his face. "I don't know what to say." The words came slowly and laboriously. "I acted like a darned fool that night and —uh—I'm sorry."

So there it was—the thing Cindy had thought would never happen, the words she had thought she would never hear. An apology from Mack! What was wrong with her? Why was it that she felt absolutely nothing?

The silence grew and she continued to stare at Mack's flushed face, his embarrassed eyes, his shining hair. And all at once she knew why his apology was meaningless. Mack's belief in her had come too late. He should have trusted her in the first place, as Peter Holmes had trusted her, without requiring proof.

The thought of Peter brought with it a sudden, inexplicable desire to see him. Cindy glanced at her watch and saw that it was only four-thirty. If Peter had stayed after school to work on the paper, he might still be in the library. If she hurried, there was an outside chance that she might find him there.

Mack leaned against the doorway and crossed his feet. His face was gradually losing its embarrassed flush. "Well, how about it?" he asked. "Going to let me out of the doghouse?"

"You're already out," Cindy replied. "As far as I'm concerned, that date we had is forgotten."

He returned his handkerchief to his pocket. "Thanks, Cindy. For a minute there, you had me worried. But I'm going to do more than apologize. I'm going to do everything possible to make up for—"

"There's nothing to make up," Cindy interrupted quickly.

"Oh, but there is." Mack was his usual confident self now. "Even if there weren't, I happen to think you're a darned cute girl and I'd like to take you out again. Shall we make it tomorrow night? I'll take you anywhere you say—even Gorley's. All you have to do is name it."

"I'm sorry. Afraid I'm going to be busy tomorrow night."

"What about Wednesday night?"

"Sorry." She shook her head and again glanced at her watch.

Mack's face fell. "You're still sore at me!"

"No, honestly, Mack, I'm not sore." Cindy smiled to show him that she meant it. "But I am very busy this week. In fact," she began to edge away from him, "I should be on my way this minute. There's something I have to take care of in the library."

"Oh." Mack's smooth, handsome face was almost funny in its look of mingled disbelief and disappointment. "Can't we even make a date for this weekend?"

"I'd rather not." Cindy made her voice gentle, trying to let him down painlessly.

Mack stared at her for a moment longer and then, with characteristic nonchalance, he shrugged. "I get it.

Never let it be said that I don't know a brush-off when I hear one. Well, let me know if you ever change your mind."

"I will," Cindy promised, turning toward the stairs. But she knew that she never would. She didn't know exactly when it had happened, and she couldn't have explained it if she'd tried, but sometime during the last few minutes her infatuation with Mack had ended, as irrationally as it had begun.

CHAPTER

20

FATE MUST HAVE BEEN SMILING on Cindy that afternoon for, when she reached the library, Peter was still there. As she crossed over to the table, he held up a stack of papers. "Glad to see you, Cindy. Several stories were turned in this afternoon and, as usual, some of them will have to be rewritten."

"All right." Cindy took the papers and glanced at them briefly. "However, that's not why I'm here. If you have a few minutes to spare, I have something to tell you."

"Never too busy for my number-one assistant." Peter put down his pencil. His hair was ruffled and there was a faint carbon smudge on his chin. "Pull out a chair and let's have it."

Cindy took the seat he'd indicated. "Well, I thought

you might like to know that I've stopped being a timid mouse!"

"You've had a talk with Rose?"

"A few minutes ago. I ran into her in the corridor and, on the spur of the moment, decided to have everything out with her once and for all."

"Good for you." Peter nodded approvingly. "How did it go?"

"Better than I thought it would. At least Rose finally admitted that her friend, the one who originally told her about the Exeter scandal, hadn't been sure of her facts."

"Nice going." Peter nodded again.

"I couldn't make her agree to do anything about the gossip, though," Cindy continued. "She made light of it and seemed to think that I should, too."

"I'm not surprised." Peter smiled reassuringly. "But don't worry, Cindy. I'd already decided that if Rose refused to set everybody straight, I'd take care of that detail myself."

"Thanks, but I don't think it will be necessary."

"But I thought you said—"

"I did, but I haven't told you everything that happened. You see, Rose and I were standing in the corridor just outside the gym when we had our argument and, as luck would have it, Mack was in the gym at the time and he heard every word we said. And when Rose told me point-blank that she wouldn't do anything, Mack came out and told her off and said that if she didn't tell everyone the truth, he would!"

"Hurray for Mack!" Peter's heartiness sounded somewhat forced. "How did Rose take it?"

"You should have seen her. When she saw that Mack meant it, she was so eager to get back in his good graces, she'd have promised anything."

"Fine." Peter was silent for a moment. "Rose is unpredictable, though, and she may change her mind. To be on the safe side, maybe I'd still better talk to some of the kids."

"That's what Mack said, too. But I don't honestly think it will be necessary for either of you to do anything more. Rose knows that the truth is going to come out now, one way or another, and, unless I miss my guess, she'll want to beat you and Mack to the punch. If she breaks the news first, she can cover up better."

"You're probably right." Peter picked up one of the books, frowned at it as though he had never seen it before, and put it down again. "I take it, then, that you and Mack had a private chat."

"Yes, we did." A little embarrassed, Cindy also picked up one of the books and pretended to examine its cover. "And Mack was very nice. He apologized for the way he behaved on that date we had and offered to do everything he could to make up for it. In fact, he asked me for another date."

"Swell!" said Peter. But his voice was so odd that Cindy couldn't help glancing swiftly up at him again.

Peter's expression was also odd. He was smiling, but it was a set, strained-looking smile which didn't extend beyond his mouth. His eyes, Cindy noticed, were unusually somber.

He brushed back his wayward lock of hair. "I know how much an apology from Mack means to you, Cindy, and I'm glad, for your sake, that it happened. Looks as though everything's going to turn out exactly as you wanted it."

So Peter had known all along how she felt about Mack! Cindy fingered her charm bracelet self-consciously. "To tell the truth, Mack's apology didn't mean as much to me as I thought it would."

Peter's grin was replaced by a quick look of amazement. "How so?"

"I guess it came too late," Cindy said slowly. "I couldn't help thinking that he should have believed in me in the first place, as you did. Anyway, I turned him down."

"I see." Peter was silent again. "You're going to retaliate by keeping him guessing for a while, is that the idea?"

"No, it's not that. I'm through with guessing games." Cindy hesitated, flushed, and fastened her gaze on a pile of manuscripts on one corner of the table. "It's sort of hard to explain, Peter, but, sometime while Mack and I were having our talk, I guess I stopped looking at him through rose-colored glasses and saw him as he really is. Anyway, I realize now that there's as much difference between Mack and me as there is between Rose and me. We don't even *think* alike. And, knowing that, I don't feel the same about him."

"Say that again?"

"I said that I don't feel about Mack the way that I did." Cindy's cheeks felt as though they were on fire, but she made herself go on. "I don't feel that way about anybody now." She glanced up, startled, as Peter suddenly pushed back his chair.

Peter's expression had changed completely. He was grinning again but this time there was nothing strained or artificial about his grin. It was genuine and whole-hearted—the kind of grin which made his entire face light up. Looking at him, Cindy found herself wondering how she could ever have thought he was homely.

"I can wait," he said ambiguously. Without another word, he turned and began to gather up his books and papers.

Cindy stared at him in bewilderment. "Aren't you going to do any more work?"

"Not today." Peter looked down at her again and, behind the shell-rimmed glasses, his eyes were shining. "A long time ago, Cindy, I asked you for a date and you gave me a rain check. Is it still good?"

"Yes, of course," she replied.

"That's all I wanted to know." Peter reached for his poplin jacket. His grin stretched almost from ear to ear. "Come on, Cindy, pick up your rewrites and let's get started. I'm going to take you home!"

215

Two days later, at the end of the weekly Glee Club rehearsal, Martha and Jan and Susan asked Cindy to go down to Weyman's with them.

"We have something important to say to you," Martha explained.

"Please say yes," begged Susan. "If you don't, I won't be able to sleep a wink tonight."

"Neither will I," said Jan.

From the way all three girls were behaving, Cindy had a fairly good idea of what was coming. Rose, she thought to herself, had evidently not wasted too much time. "I'll be glad to go downtown with you," she said, smiling.

Ten minutes later, the foursome were seated in one of Weyman's booths. For a while, they talked about commonplace things, and none of Cindy's three companions seemed to want to come to the point. But finally Susan said, "The sooner we get it over with, the better we'll feel! You start, Martha."

Martha nodded and turned to Cindy. "The reason we asked you to come here with us today, Cindy, is that we owe you an apology. We— Well, there was some gossip about you going around, a few weeks ago. The story was that you'd tried to elope with a college boy when you were living in Exeter, and we didn't have any better sense than to listen to it and believe it."

"Yes, I know," Cindy said quietly.

"You've heard the story?" asked Susan.

"Only recently," Cindy replied.

The three girls looked at each other. Jan coughed nervously. "What we're trying to say is that we know now that there wasn't a word of truth in the story, and we're sorry we ever believed it. I'm afraid that we've been awfully unfair to you."

"The hard part," Cindy said slowly, "was not knowing what was wrong. You see, for a long time I *didn't* know about the gossip and I couldn't understand why everyone was snubbing me. If I'd actually been guilty, I'd probably have guessed what was going on, but as it was I had no idea. And I was beginning to imagine all sorts of things about myself." She turned to Martha. "How did you find out that the gossip wasn't true?"

"Rose Walsh told me this morning." Martha's ordinarily pink cheeks were pale. "It seems that it was Rose who originally started the gossip. She'd heard it from a friend of hers who lives near Exeter. Then, only yesterday, Rose received a letter from her friend saying that she'd just learned that you weren't the girl involved in the Exeter scandal, after all."

Cindy grinned in spite of herself. Trust Rose to find an easy way out!

"Honestly, Cindy, I'm so ashamed of myself I don't know what to do!" Susan blurted. "I wish you'd bawl me out or something!"

"I feel the same way," said Jan. "But if it will make you feel better, Cindy, at least we've learned something from this. We talked it all over at noon and we've decided that we're never again going to listen to or repeat gossip of any kind."

"Even if the story had been true and you *had* been the girl," Martha said in a troubled voice, "we shouldn't have treated you as we did. We're old enough to know that everyone makes mistakes. Being unfair to you was one of *our* mistakes. But we made it and all we can do now is tell you how sorry we are and ask you to forgive us. Won't you, please?"

Cindy gazed at the three anxious faces surrounding her. These were the girls she had liked so much on first acquaintance and, in her heart, she liked them still. They'd hurt her, yes, but thoughtlessly rather than deliberately. And hadn't she made mistakes, too? She smiled first at Martha, then at Susan, and then at Jan.

"Of course I forgive you," she said. "Actually it's as much my fault as yours."

"How could it be your fault?" asked Jan.

"Well, since we're letting our hair down," Cindy began. She told them about her dissatisfaction with herself in Exeter and about the magazine article which had inspired her decision to make herself over into a new person. "But I guess I overdid it," she finished. "It was all right to try to improve my appearance but I shouldn't have pretended to be something that I'm not!" She paused, coloring. "To give you an idea of what I'm really like, I'll tell you what they called me in Exeter, if you'll promise not to tell anyone else."

"Cross my heart," Martha said solemnly.

"Almost everyone there called me 'Beanpole'!" Cindy confessed.

"Beanpole!" Martha repeated, and there was a chorus of giggles.

"I think it's sort of cute," said Jan.

Cindy glanced at her suspiciously. "Promise you won't tell anyone!"

"I won't breathe it to a soul."

"I'll make a bargain with you, Cindy," said Susan. "I'll promise not to reveal your deep, dark secret if you'll promise to help us with our knitting. You told me that you knew how, remember?"

"Yes, I remember." Cindy's eyes met Susan's and she knew that the memory was as painful to Susan as it was to her. She smiled quickly. "And I'll be glad to help.

"While we're on the subject of Exeter," she continued, "there's something I forgot to tell you. I do have a very good friend there named Sally Baird. I've been thinking that I'd like to invite her down for a visit soon and perhaps have a party for her—to introduce her to some of the Woodmont kids. I know you'd like her. She paused, struck by a sudden inspiration. "Why don't I call her tonight and invite her down for this weekend? We could have the party Saturday night."

"Sounds like a wonderful idea to me," said Martha.

"Me, too," Jan agreed.

"I'd love to come!" Susan cried enthusiastically. "We

could invite all of the would-be knitters and maybe you could give us our first lesson. Or do you think it would be nicer if we had boys?"

Cindy glanced shyly around the table. "It might be more fun if we invited boys, too. In fact, there's one boy I want very much to invite."

Susan groaned. "Mack Gordon, I suppose. Oh well, if it will make you happy, I'll try to get along with him for one evening."

"Who said anything about Mack Gordon?" Cindy retorted, grinning. "I'm talking about Peter Holmes!"